STILL RIVER

A NOVEL

DAWN PAUL

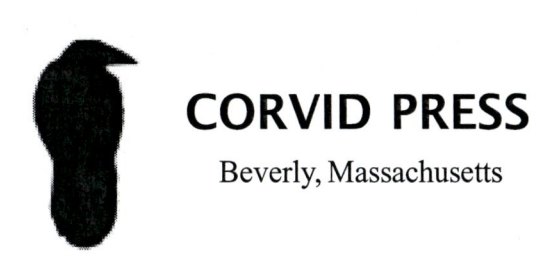

CORVID PRESS
Beverly, Massachusetts

Copyright © 2006 by Dawn Paul

This is a work of fiction. Any resemblance to actual persons or places is entirely coincidental.

Chapters of this book have been published, in slightly different form, as follows:
"Outliers" has appeared in the journal Earth's Daughters
"The Hawk" has appeared online at *Storyglossia.com*
"One Clean Pain" was part of Adam Leveille's art installation of the same title

Cover art and design by Ben Johnson
www.wanderingcrow.com

ISBN-13: 978-0-9744965-1-1
ISBN-10: 0-9744965-1-0

CORVID PRESS   2 Lovett Court
Beverly, Massachusetts
01915
www.corvidpress.com

The author is grateful to the writing community that made this book possible, especially Rebecca Brown, Jan Clausen, Marilyn McLatchey, Susan Newell, Ellen Orleans, Joan Powers, Elizabeth Rollins, Kirsten Rybczynski and Christine Simokaitis.

Thank you also to Wellspring House for a quiet place to write.

This book is for Marilyn.

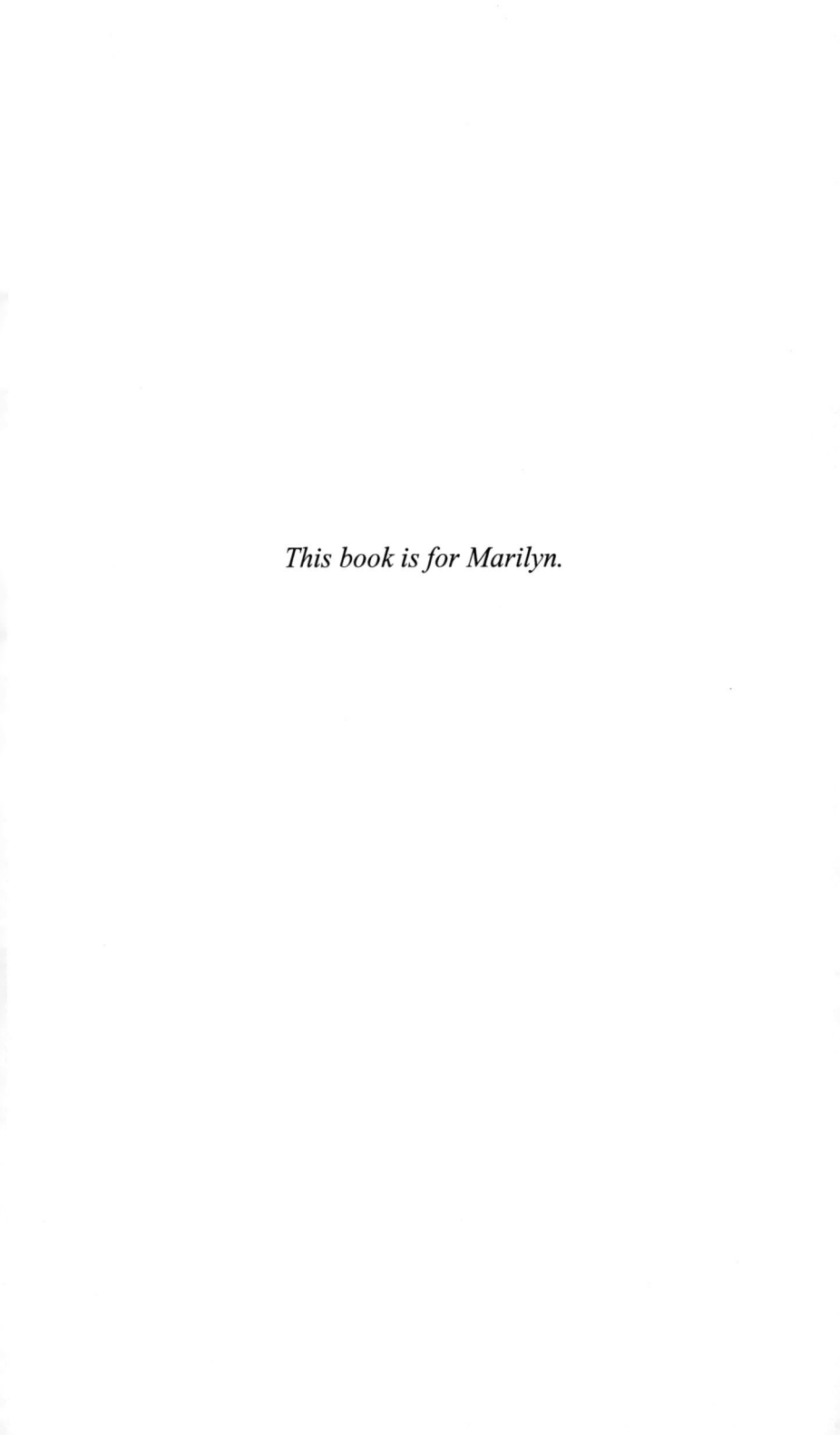

Still River

From the Beginning	11
Under the Ice	13
Winter Ecology	17
The River Rises	21
The Hatch-out	26
Still River, Fall	30
The Blue Globe	35
Still River, Winter	42
One Clean Pain	45
The Bridge	47
Thermal Memory	48
The Riverine Environment	57
The Swimming Place	59
Cedar Waxwings	62
The Out-of-Season Deer	68
The Hawk	77
The Heron Path	85
Snow Geese	90
The Nivean Environment	99
Spring Thaw	107
Under the Bridge	108
Sorting	112
Leaving	118
Wilderness	121
Outliers	124
Baptism	127
Reservoir	131

From the Beginning

If you look at a map of southern New England, you will see a broad flat area south of where the White Mountains veer west into New York to eventually join the Adirondacks. In that inland plain, glaciers left a series of ponds and lakes—Singletary, Suntaug, Wakefield, Wallum, Holton's Hollow—that mark the smooth landscape like holes worn in old cloth. These ponds and lakes are linked by rivers that carry meltwater from the mountains in a southeasterly direction to Narragansett Bay and Rhode Island Sound.

The Still River is one of the more southerly of these rivers. It runs generally east across central Rhode Island, draining Carrick's Pond, which is more correctly a swamp. After twelve miles, it forks into King's River, which flows south, and the Pawtuxet River, which widens and continues east to the Bay. The Still River was named, not for calm waters, but for the Still family that farmed and grazed sheep along its banks for several generations beginning in the mid-1600s. In time, the Still family branched out to other parts of the country, leaving their properties to families with more optimism than daring. To the Palmers, Greenes, Goodnoughs and Slaters that followed, Eben Still's river became the Still River.

Contrary to what most people believe, the landscape of southern New England in the teeming mid-twentieth century had more forest than it did in the earlier nineteenth century. The land through which the Still River flows typifies that change. By the end of the nineteenth century, most farmers in the area had discovered what the Still family had found long before: there were better ways to make a living than plowing stones in New England. Families let open fields lie fallow and moved to cities or the Midwest. The trees crept back, sending out pioneer species like cedar and birch, and eventually forming a mixed hardwood forest. By the 1960s, the Still River was again, in a way it had not been since the 1600s, a wilderness. Though mapped and crossed by bridges, it was wilderness in the sense that it was uncultivated, unsettled and populated by wild animals.

In that margin of political time between the publication of Rachel Carson's *Silent Spring* and the first celebration of Earth Day, the Still River was remarkably clean for an eastern river. Upstream pollution was largely filtered by swathes of rushes in Carrick's Pond, and the Still's remote location had discouraged the building of textile or leather mills along its banks. So, while the Still River was not pristine, its waters were pure enough to consider impounding for a reservoir. Another land-hungry population was once again encroaching on the forest—real estate developers. Their customers would need water. The river and its surrounding lowlands were extensively surveyed in the late 1960s, and the privately owned lands that would be inundated by the reservoir were taken by eminent domain in 1968.

In that same year, a sixteen-year-old boy named David Brownell drowned in the Still River. It was winter, and his body was carried under the ice until it surfaced in an open stretch of water three-and-a-half miles downstream. There he was found by Jay Bruley, a girl who later befriended his sister, Eleanor.

This is the story of all of them: David, Jay, Eleanor and the river.

Under the Ice

1
Go ahead. Do it.
No. Winter. Freezing just standing here. Ice downriver.
What would it feel like, just diving in?
Cold.
Hey guys I went swimming yesterday. Yeah. Down at the river. Bet your ass it was cold. Yeah. I could tell them that. Hey Dave. He's okay that Dave.
Do it. Yeah I can do this.
No. Way too cold. My nuts will freeze.
Can that really happen?
Bet it's just cold for a minute. Then you get warm. Get used to it. Do it.
I'm so hot. Inside. I don't know what I want. Ever.
I don't want to think about it anymore.
It was like I'd been waiting for something.
It was like it was the first time someone really looked at me.
It was like I saw my life going forward, getting wider, like headlights on a back road.
Stupid.
I'm nothing special.
I'm like that guy that delivers the oil for the furnace. He drives up, unwinds the big hose on the back of the truck, sticks the nozzle down the fill pipe on the side of the house. Then just stands there. Waiting. Back to the truck, pushes a button and the hose rewinds. It's always the same guy. Skinny. Navy blue pants and shirt. The shirt's got a patch on the front. DuBois Bros. Heating Oil. Just like it says on

the truck. But he's not a DuBois brother. In winter, they give him a navy blue jacket.

When he comes to the door with the bill, he smells like oil. Like the basement smells for a few days after the delivery. He's got oil rubbed into the pores on his face and the skin around his fingernails.

That's me. A skinny guy who doesn't even have his own smell.

And then we were crossing the river. Right here.

I want to stop things that have already happened.

I want to wash it all away.

One clean pain.

Wouldn't that feel good?

Jezzus, I'm cold just standing here. It's starting to snow. Like bits of ice.

Looks so clean. Every stone on the bottom speckled and sharp. Bottle cap. Not even rusty. Cold must kill everything. All the weeds and scum.

Just take off your clothes. Jump. Quick. Don't even think.

Cold.

Don't think.

One clean pain.

Fingers are numb already. Funny, watching them, can't feel them, watching them pull that zipper like it was someone else's fingers.

Don't think.

My jockeys laying in the snow. Now that's a sight you don't think a guy's ever going to see. Funny as hell.

Cold.

One clean pain.

I can't do this.

Don't think.

One.   Two.   Three.

2
Winter baptism. I take him down, his hot white body, pearls of air pouring from his mouth. His eyes stare wide at the clean gravel, blue irises like the inside of a shell, the stun of frigid water in that nacreous look.

His neck gleams hard and white, incised with the faint rings that foretell good fortune. A trail of pale freckles across fragile shoulders, those long nicked shins.

They decide when they are ready. I am always here.

This time, cradling the boy, reaching in to slow his wild heart. He pulls me in and I fill his mouth, throat, lungs. I fill his ears and lie close to the brain that is frantically diving deeper to the core that remembers breathing liquid.

He rises, his body cools, bony fingers and toes spread like fins. I swirl him over in my current. Water laps up his ribcage and pools in the taut hollow of his belly. He drifts, comes to rest at the edge of the ice. I hold him on his back, open to the gray sky, hair tugged back gently by the current. Snowflakes gather on his forehead like a cool hand laid across a fever.

I suck him under the lip of the ice, run a tongue of ripples down his cold belly and thighs and carry him along. Past turtles sleeping under river-steeped leaves. Open-lipped clams drinking the cold. A drowsy trout turns a dull eye to this long white sight sliding downstream. And at the bend, a muskrat den throws mammal warmth like a lantern on an old road to guide you home.

3
A girl downriver leans to toss a coin
over the ice, with a whispered wish,

into a dark green swirl of water.
What can I do, but take the coin and the wish,
under the ice, with that rare sweet swimmer,
under the ice, toward the sea?

4
Eleanor? Welcome to the nivean environment.
But it's so cold outside.

Winter Ecology

"Contrary to popular belief," Professor Shapiro said, "a person who falls into cold water—I'm talking zero centigrade—does not die quickly. It takes a good ten minutes for the body's core temperature to even begin to drop. There are instances where an individual submerged in cold water has survived for two hours."

For the first time in years, maybe since the day, Eleanor deliberately thought about David's death. Not the fact that he was dead. That thought came to mind an average of once a day. But his actual death in the river. She had always thought of it as quick—imagined the near-freezing water closing over his head, his pulse rate dropping, darkness.

Professor Shapiro moved back to hard science. Temperature gradients, stratification. Did David have time to struggle? To change his mind as the current pulled him away? There was good research out there on cold water submersion. Eleanor needed to find it.

Shapiro danced across the front of the room, filling the board with equations. He was enthusiastic, as though he had derived those equations—basic thermodynamics, really—just that morning. He moved fast, bounding from physics to field studies to anecdotes about his work with the Army in the Arctic. Eleanor lost track, thinking about David in the river, and knew she would never catch up. She would have to catch him after class to fill in her missing notes. He was always happy to be on his favorite subjects and she knew he would be delighted to explain it all over again. He would ask her name again, too, as though his class was a lecture hall intro course and not a ten-student graduate seminar.

Eleanor kept thinking of David, looking back at the shore. She wanted to get up and walk across campus, find the research, and figure it out. David had been fragile and thin-skinned, bony and pale like a newly hatched sparrow. She tended to think of him as taller and older than her. But when she looked at sixteen-year-old boys pushing each other along the sidewalks in town, she knew he had been young.

Shapiro began talking about latent cooling and ice. Ice. The river was iced over that year. David would have been sucked under the ice by the current. Drowned. No time to struggle. Eleanor let out a sigh of relief. The student next to her — Jim? Tim? — tilted his notebook so that she could see it, taking her sigh as frustration with the calculations. She waved him off, then remembered to smile. He was trying to help.

After class, she followed Professor Shapiro to his office. He cleared notebooks off a chair and motioned for her to sit down. Then he moved a pile of papers to make room for his briefcase. Eleanor could not imagine working in that confusion. She had loved chemistry, her undergraduate major, mostly because it was orderly and logical. Each side of the equation always balanced.

Professor Shapiro's winter ecology seminar was known on campus as a fruit and nuts course. But it was a relatively new area and offered a lot of research opportunities. There was field work and time spent tramping around in Wyoming's high country with thermometers and core sampling gear. Shapiro liked to throw new findings at his students. Like that morning's tidbit on the survival rate of ice water immersion victims.

"Eleanor Brownell?" he said tentatively. He had large dark eyes and with his shaggy beard that sprouted high on his cheekbones, he reminded her of the bison that the agriculture department had penned on the outskirts of campus. They had that same troubled and kindly look.

Eleanor explained that she had gotten behind in his lecture. Without any reprimand, he launched into his equations again, sketching them out on the cover of what looked like a talk he planned to give at next week's geophysical conference. When he finished, he sat back and tugged at his thick dark beard.

"Eleanor, you have a fine scientific mind." He said this like it was a grim diagnosis. "You have the ability to break things down into their simplest parts. Reduce it all," he gestured at the disarray of his office, "to data points." He looked at her with his kind bison eyes. "To be successful in the ecology field, you're going to have to turn that way of thinking upside-down. Learn to see the effect of the whole on the individual even while you are examining the individual."

"Are you saying I'm in the wrong field?"

"Not at all, not at all. I think you'll be very successful. Your field work is excellent. Very detailed. I'm just saying that you need to...consider more. Not be in such a rush to nail down a hypothesis. If anyone gathers enough data, they can always form some sort of conclusion. But is the conclusion always the important thing?"

"Well, isn't that the point of science, Dr. Shapiro? To find answers?"

"Dan. When people call me Doctor, I look around for my father. He was an opthalmologist. You have some intriguing questions in your work with thermoclines in large bodies of water."

"And I'm getting some good answers."

He smiled and shook his dark shaggy head.

Twenty years later, Eleanor was Dr. Brownell and still asking questions about thermoclines in large bodies of water. She was still learning about the effect of the whole on the individual. And still thinking about her brother

David, who jumped into a river in mid-winter. Her long-ago logical conclusion, that he drowned under the ice long before the onset of hypothermia, never did answer the original question: Did he struggle?

The River Rises

"Where are you from, Jay?"

Jay usually told people that she moved around, all over New England. Talking made her tired and she didn't tell long stories. But when this girl asked, in her soft North Carolina way of talking, Jay had an urge to tell her about the Still River and the reservoir. Maybe because she was, like Jay, a scholarship student. Or because Jay had seen her buying art supplies at the hardware store in town. Neither of them could afford the little art shop on campus. Things like that shouldn't matter at an art school, but they did.

So Jay told her about the years it took to create the Still River Reservoir. How, long before they built the dam, the state took her family's land by eminent domain. They surveyed and planned and for three years the Bruleys lived on their land as renters. It broke her father. A slow breaking.

Finally, the state condemned the house and the outbuildings and brought in the bulldozers. It was another year before the dam was completed and the water started rising. Jay and her family were living up north by then and it didn't matter. But when she looked back on it, she saw that the water had been rising up around the Bruley family for quite a while.

By the time they condemned the house, Jay's oldest brother Wes had already left home and was working timber up north with their Uncle Leon. The day the surveyors condemned the house, Uncle Leon called Pa, shouting so loud into the phone that Jay and her brother Dale could hear him clear across the kitchen.

"Bring Dale and the girl up here now, Clement. Don't wait 'til the water's up to your knees, for Godsake." At least the Bruleys had a place to go.

Where did everyone else go? Pete Slater, who had been born on his farm. The herons that roosted in the willow thickets by the river. The sun turtles. The black beetles that crazied around in the shallows.

Before he lost his land, Pa took Jay with him to one of the town hearings on the reservoir. He told her that, at the age of twelve, she was old enough to appreciate local democracy. Wes and Dale, though older, had no interest in going to the hearings. Just a lot of talking, they said, and Pa let them stay home.

As they drove into town that night, Pa said, "You might hear some harsh talk tonight, Jay. People aren't going to give up their place without a fight. Some of these families have been on their land since it belonged to the King of England."

They got to the Town Hall and a woman in spike high heels led them down a long corridor. Her shoes made so much noise that Jay expected someone to come out of one of the closed doors and shush them. She stopped and pointed to a door with a frosted glass window.

"Right in there, Mr. Bruley." She gave Jay a thin smile and hammered her way back down the hall.

Inside the room, a man with a plaid shirt tucked into stiff new work pants was taping big drawings up on the wall. A dozen people sat around a long wooden table sipping coffee from paper cups and handing each other folders and papers. They were talking loudly, as though they were the only people in the room. A thin bald man kept rearing back in his chair and letting out a big snorting laugh like a horse.

Everyone else—Jay and her father, Pete Slater, her Uncle Armand and Auntie Pauline, the Plickerts, old Mrs. Palmer—stood in the back. Uncle Armand left the room and came back with a folding chair for Mrs. Palmer. The man in the plaid wool shirt used a long pointing stick to trace the curving lines of the river on one of the big sheets of paper. He showed where the dam would be built. He pointed to another piece of paper and explained how the river would rise and fill the natural valley of the Still River. Jay pictured it like water cupped in someone's hands. He talked about flow rates, budgets and timetables.

Finally, Pa stepped forward and said, "So when's all this supposed to get started?"

The man lowered his stick and looked down the table at everyone whose land would be in the cupped hands of the reservoir. His eyes held Pa's for a second then slid away. "It's started, Mr. Bruley. You'll be receiving a notice pertaining to your property any day now."

The people sitting around the table shifted like dogs getting settled on a warm thick rug. The room went quiet. Then Mrs. Palmer scraped back her chair and stood up stiffly. She turned and walked out of the room. Everyone else followed. Jay asked no questions on the way home and her father offered no answers.

There was an old graveyard on Pete Slater's place tucked into a corner of a hayfield. The big headstones were brittle and dark. Years of frost and thaw had set them a-kilter. They had old-time names carved in them—Elisha, Hepzibah, Ephraim. The children's stones were small white nubbins pushing up out of the dirt like puppy teeth. Most of the stones had just a name and two dates. Wes had taught Jay how to count back the years to figure people's ages when they died. The oldest was Nehemias Slater, ninety-six years, three months. Baby Ann lasted just three days. Her sister Dorcas died two days later at one year, ten months. February, 1842.

Right after they condemned Pete Slater's farm, they moved the graveyard. They dug up the old coffins and bones and re-buried them in a big flat green cemetery across town. The next day, Jay walked up to the field where it had been. They had pushed over one side of the stone wall to get the backhoe in. A pattern of tire treads like a big zipper showed where the backhoe had been ridden back and forth across the ground to make it smooth. There were chunks of pale gray clay, the clay that runs deep in the ground, mixed with the dark topsoil. The ground looked soft, as though Jay would sink in up to her hips if she jumped over the tumbledown wall.

Pete Slater hadn't wanted them to move his old relations. He said if they were going to take and flood his land they might as well flood the bones and everything else that came with it. But they explained that people would not want to drink water that had dead bodies under it.

Jay was glad her mother was buried with her own people up in Quebec. Sometimes Jay used to wish that she could sit by her mother's grave, to see if she could feel her spirit, the way Pete Slater could stand in the middle of his gathered dead. That day, Jay looked at the clods of gray clay tamped down into the earth, at the uprooted birch sapling lying alongside the wall, and was glad her mother was not buried on the Bruley's land.

In the end, Jay's family did not take much with them. And, in the end, Jay finally saw her father's anger.

They came one November morning and nailed signs to the biggest pines and oaks, the sheds, the barn, everything that would be bulldozed. They nailed a sign to the porch post, and when they did, their hammering knocked an old phoebe nest from under the porch roof. The phoebe had been finding her way back to her nesting spot for years whether the old nest remained or not. A winter storm could have done as much damage. In any event, when the phoebe returned in spring, the house would be gone, razed to the ground. Jay's father knew this.

He picked up the fallen nest, carried it across the yard to where one of the surveyors stood leafing through papers on a clipboard. The surveyor was young-looking and wore owlish eyeglasses. He smiled at her father, who up until then had been calm and polite. Pete Slater had tried to run them over with his tractor.

Her father shook the nest in the young surveyor's face and cursed him. Then he grabbed the clipboard from the man, who stood with his head tilted to one side, blinking behind his glasses in amazement. Her father broke the clipboard over the fence rail. Papers blew across the road, through the pine grove and down the slope to the thickets. They may have blown all the way down to the river, for all Jay knew or cared.

Six days later, they moved north. The moving around part of Jay's life started. Jay remembered Cara saying it was a sad story. But Jay hadn't told her the saddest part. The part she still remembered, twenty years later, so clearly. Eleanor Brownell.

The Hatch-out

It rained for nine days. Rain ripped the petals off Mrs. Castelli's tulip tree and beat the orchard's renegade daffodils into the mud. Eleanor lay on her bed with a book about deserts and tried to imagine a world without water. David listened to music in his room. The closets smelled like mildew. The car wouldn't start because the wires were wet and their mother restlessly patrolled the kitchen and living room. They ate their meals one at a time, as though the kitchen was too small to hold all three of them in a streak of bad weather.

On Sunday it stopped raining. Their mother insisted that David could get the car started. Eleanor stood at the back door and watched him poke at the engine with a rag while their mother stood with her pocketbook and coat over her arm.

Eleanor slipped out the door and went walking towards the river, into the woods where everything still dripped and oozed. She found a dark pool deep with new rain. Along the shallow edges of the pool, shapeless masses of pale green frog eggs hung in the cold water. Each mass was full of single eggs, like clear green peas. In the middle of each egg there was a black pinhead of a tadpole in a dark moss-green sack.

Eleanor ran her fingers through the frog eggs, gently to not break them apart, and they flowed past her hand cold as the water itself. At one end of the pool, sunlight fell on another soft mass of pale green. This one had black specks floating just under the surface. Eleanor knelt down to look. They were tadpole hatchlings. Each was the size of the white half-moon of her little fingernail, but wriggling with a complete head and finned tail. As she watched, one slid out of a green sack and instantly became part of the squiggly black mass of new tadpoles. There were thousands. Eleanor knelt on the wet ground and watched. One after another, the hatchlings slid out of their wet globules of green, each a slip of a someday frog.

A bluejay called as it flew over and she looked up. She had been so intent on the tiny world of green that the woods seemed huge. The tadpoles would soon be gone, this whole world that had been happening all morning while she brushed her teeth and put on her socks. She stood and ran back up the path, slipping on last year's dead leaves, wanting to show it all to someone. She reached the street and slowed to a trot. Mr. Boudreau was scrubbing his tires with a brush. Mrs. Castelli waved from her porch and Eleanor was ready to run and tell her about the hatch-out but she went back inside. She reached her own house still breathing hard from running and was relieved to see that the car was gone.

The house smelled like hot cocoa and airplane glue. David was in the living room, sitting cross-legged on the couch sticking clear cellophane insignia on a model airplane. He soaked them in water to soften the glue, then gently lifted them out on the tip of his finger, one at a time, and placed them on a wing of the plane.

"David!"

He raised one wet finger. "Just a sec."

"There's something I need to show you."

"Now? Have some cocoa."

"It has to be now. It's happening now."

He sighed and set the plane carefully on the coffee table. Then he followed her out the door. She ran ahead of him to make him hurry. He walked with his hands in his pockets, blinking in the sharp sunlight. She led him down the path to the pool and motioned him to the edge of the water.

"What?"

"A hatch-out. Tadpoles. Look."

"Those little black things? Creepy."

"If we came down here yesterday or tomorrow, we would have missed it!"

"What's the green slime?"

"Egg masses."

"Holy shit. There's millions of them." David stood rocking from foot to foot as though he was cold. He looked up the path. "Sure are a lot of them."

Eleanor knew he wanted to go back to the house. He got cold easily because he was so thin, and he wasn't wearing a jacket. He looked at her and smiled, nodded at the tadpoles. But Eleanor knew he didn't really care and was thinking of airplane wings and stars. David, at least, would stand and look. But no one really cared. She looked down at the thousands of hatchlings and felt an ache start up in her throat and tears in her eyes.

"Ellie? What's the matter?"

She couldn't answer because her throat was choking and because she didn't know. She wiped her eyes on her jacket sleeve and watched the tadpoles in their happy wiggling until the tears came up again to blur them.

"Look at that one, Ellie, making his getaway. Must of stole something. That one looks like he's dancing, doesn't he? It looks like the last day of school, doesn't it? All the kids out in front of the school, everyone happy. Looking forward to being big frogs next year."

Eleanor sniffled and giggled. The tadpoles did look like kids let loose for the summer. David smiled, but still looked worried. He bent down to look into her face.

"They'll be fine, Ellie. They're gonna be okay."

Eleanor knew most of them would get eaten. Turtles, birds, snakes—everyone had to eat. That was the amazing thing, that there would be so many and only two or three would make it to be frogs. The only protection they had was their huge wriggling numbers. But she did not tell that to David. If he thought they were going to have fun all summer and grow up to be frogs, she did not want to tell him the truth.

He rubbed at the goosebumps rising up on his arms and Eleanor said that they should head back home. They started up the path. Then David stopped and pulled at her sleeve.

"Ellie, look."

She turned and saw that a small green-backed heron had landed by the pool and was already stabbing at the water. David grabbed a stick and cocked his arm back to throw it at the heron.

"No. Leave it."

"But you were just crying about them and—"

"It's okay, leave it."

He shook his head and laughed, then tossed the stick into the woods.

Still River, Fall

It was the smell of the wine that made David pass the bottle to Mike without drinking. It was the memory of home. His mother's glass on the kitchen table in the morning. He watched Mike, Aaron the new kid, then Kev, in the light of the fire. Watched them swig, wipe their lips with the back of their hands and pass the bottle along. Black trees closed around them. But David was not afraid. When the bottle came around again, he drank. The rim of the bottle was warm and slick on his lips. The wine was sweet and burned all the way to his belly. This was not home.

They were sitting on the gravel bank by the river. Mike had started a fire. It was early September, hot days and cold nights. David watched a satellite track across the sky above the trees across the river. The four of them sat, not talking. David listened to the river, the sticks popping in the fire and distant cars.

He was not home. The boys' sweet wine opened up the night to vague pleasant possibilities. David could feel the possibilities and they were mixed up with the heat of the fire and the wine. We could be anywhere, he thought. Out in the night, in another country, just the four of us. The river sounds were loud in the dark.

"Listen to the river. Doesn't it sound like music?" It could be a mistake, David knew. Talking could be a mistake.

"Dave, sometimes you are such a fuckin' airhead, man." Kev kicked David's foot toward the fire. No, Kev would not want to talk about music in the river. Kev wanted to talk about things he already knew.

"It does sound like music. Like when the Dead get jamming or something." So Mike was not going to let Kev shove them into a typical Friday night. David smiled. He wanted to reach over, put his hand on Mike's shoulder and say...what? He raised his head and realized that he was feeling the wine. Aaron was looking across the fire at him.

"The river sounds like jazz to me. You guys listen to jazz at all?" Aaron didn't stop for the answer. "It's like that. The sound just keeps going, keeps blending and breaking apart. You have to stay with it. Pay attention or it stops making sense." It was the most David had heard Aaron say. He was new. His family had moved in a few weeks ago, just before school started. He had shown up tonight with Mike carrying four bottles of wine. He looked older. Probably could buy without getting carded. Tall, with close-cut dark hair. Kev said he was Jewish.

Mike opened up another bottle and passed it to Aaron. David watched his throat move as he drank. Aaron's neck and jaw had a hard spareness. In the light of the fire, his face was all sharp-edged. He was clean-shaven. He had none of the boyish roundness that the others covered with tufts of beard. David rubbed his own thin gingery sideburns. Aaron, David decided, would be the only one of them who could survive a plane crash. He would walk out of the jungle six weeks after the crash when everyone had given up on survivors.

"Do any of you play?" Aaron asked.

"Play what?" Kev wore his stupidity like a medal.

"Music. An instrument. I play flute. I started with clarinet and oboe in orchestra, but I've been playing flute lately. I had a jazz quartet going before we moved."

"My mother made us take piano," Mike said. "I don't play anymore, but my sister's pretty good."

"I'm learning to play the drums," David said. He had never thought of playing music before. He had only thought of listening. Playing was something other people did. But suddenly he could see himself with drumsticks. Laying down a steady beat that went on and on like the river while Aaron blew wild notes on his flute.

"No kidding?" Mike said. "When did you start playing drums?"

"A while back. I'm not much good yet. I'm just learning." He would start tomorrow. Call Dad and ask him for money for lessons. Why not?

"My father has a collection of old jazz records. He's got some drummers. Art Blakey. Buddy Rich. You might want to come over and listen to them sometime." Aaron smiled at him across the fire. The planes of his face shifted when he smiled. He didn't look so serious and distant. He looked directly into David's eyes like he was making a promise. David smiled back, then looked away.

Kev passed him the bottle and he gulped at it. It left his mouth sour. Mike started a story about hitching to a concert. Kev broke a branch and threw the pieces into the fire. Sparks rose up and swirled. Aaron leaned his head back, watching the sparks. His jacket was open and dark hair curled at the vee of his shirt collar. Aaron looked down quickly, caught David's stare, and smiled again.

Then Aaron's face was bright in a silver beam of light and there were more lights cutting through the trees, turning them gray like ashes. Shouts came from the hill behind them. Mike crashed the bottle into the river.

"Cops!"

They jumped up, cops charging down the hill in front of them, the river behind them. David heard Mike crash into the woods. He wondered if he should try to put out the fire. He heard Kev yell "you fuckin' bastard." An answer — "I got you, you little fucker." Then Aaron was pulling him by the arm into the river and he was half swimming, half stumbling in the dark. The water was cold and he could feel the heat of Aaron's fingers digging into his arm. Then Aaron was ahead of him, a dark shape streaked with wet light.

They reached the opposite shore, running, gravel impossibly loud under their feet. They crashed up into tangled little trees, crunching dead leaves on the ground. Aaron pulled David down. His fingers dug into his arm again. They lay together in the leaves looking down at the river. The fire was still blazing on the other side and big uniforms lurched around in silver-gray cones of light.

"Get down. They'll see us." David felt the weight and heat of Aaron's hand on the back of his neck. His lips touched his ear. "You're shaking. You okay?"

"Cold." Aaron put his arm across his shoulders and David willed the shaking in his chest to draw down into a small quivery pit in his belly.

"I think they got Kev. Are the cops always like this out here? We were just drinking a little wine. It's like a police state." Aaron's mouth was against his ear, his breath warm. If I turn my head, David thought, my mouth will be next to his. He spoke down into the leaves.

"They must have thought we had a big blowout going on."

"Dave. I need to get home. I'm already real late. I'm going to head down the river and circle back to the road. If they see me, will you take off in the other direction, confuse them a little?"

"Sure. No problem." David felt Aaron shift away from him. The warm weight of his arm lifted from David's shoulders, leaving a cold strip.

"See you later, okay Dave?" David watched Aaron run in a low crouch down to the river and into the dark. Across the river, the cops were busy kicking out the fire. Some were making their way back up the hill. David could see the headlights of two cruisers blazing into the trees. His clothes were wet. He started shivering again. The cops peeled out, tires spitting gravel. David sat up and fingered a scratch across his cheek. He tasted blood on his fingertips. He felt queasy.

He was disappointed. After the wine and the fire and listening to the river, after David had seen them together playing wild music on the drums and the flute, after the promise they had made across the fire, Aaron was running home.

David picked himself up and brushed muddy leaves from his wet clothes. He blundered his way in the dark down to the river and home.

The Blue Globe

Mr. DiPietro was not like the other teachers. He did not care if kids passed notes or tilted back in their chairs. He did not seem to notice. He taught English. In the drowsy afternoons, he read to them, striding back and forth in front of the blackboard. He read in a loud voice, his book in one hand, the other waving in the air, and did not notice when kids snickered. David thought it was embarrassing, the way Mr. DiPietro read. But he never laughed. Sometimes Mr. DiPietro stopped and looked up from his book, excited and looking for excitement in the faces of his students. They sat, dreaming of mag wheels and new shoes. When he looked at David, with his face shining and hopeful, it was worse than being called on and not knowing the answer.

Today, Mr. DiPietro read poetry. It didn't make any sense, but David liked sitting with his legs stretched out under his desk while the pictures rolled over him. Burning tigers. Big shoulders. A world in your hand. He remembered the world in his hand. His six-year-old hand in the big bedroom of the first house they lived in. When they were all happy. It was summer.

The windows are open, sunlight falling in gold blocks on the wood floor. The bed wide and white behind him. He is standing in front of his mother's dresser, going through her jewelry box. He lets gold chains run through his fingers, drops a handful of earrings one by one. He slips shiny silver bracelets over his hand and piles them along his arm, shaking it to hear them jingle. Then he finds the blue glass ball. Smooth and shining, heavy in his hand. He can see himself in it, a curved face with a wide smile.

"David? What are you doing?" His father speaks quietly and David turns, ready to hold out the beautiful blue ball to him. He sees his father's face and stops.

"Take those bracelets off. Now."

Mr. DiPietro finished the last poem and stood in front of the class, eyes sparkling and expectant. The kids squirmed and stretched. David reached under his seat for his notebook. The bell rang and the kids rushed for the door, pushing and tripping over chair legs. David was thinking about the blue ball, a world in his hands. He started to walk to the front of the class, to Mr. DiPietro, who was packing his books into a worn leather bag. But someone shoved him from behind and he was carried along with everyone else out the door and into the hall.

David thought about the blue ball all the way home. The house was empty and he let himself in with the key hidden under the loose shingle. He walked down the hall. The door to his mother's bedroom was open. The room smelled sour and the blankets were heaped in the middle of the bed. There was a jewelry box on the dresser. A flat white rectangle. He was not sure if it was the same one. Someone had let a cigarette burn out on the lid, leaving a brown stain.

He lifted the lid. The box was lined with thin red velvet. He picked up a wad of tangled necklaces, pricking his finger on a pin. The blue ball was not there. Outside the window, the streetlights were on, but the driveway was still empty.

He took the box into the bathroom and set it on the vanity. He stood in front of the mirror: long pale face, straight fine hair tied back tightly, bushy red sideburns. He wet his razor and shaved the sideburns. They had always looked foolish. He took off his shirt and untied his hair, letting it fall over his shoulders. Then he untangled the necklaces and put them around his neck, fumbling with the little snickety clasps. The silver bangles were gone, but there was a bracelet, a curve of copper. He hooked it around his wrist and held his hand up to the mirror. He took it off and hooked it instead where the slight swell of his biceps tapered into his shoulder. He tightened his arm and watched the muscles roll under the copper band. He remembered Mr. DiPietro reading.

"I sing of myself," he whispered in the empty house.

Aaron's house was on a new road off Route 44. David considered hitching but decided to walk. He didn't want to get picked up by a car full of cigarette smoke. Aaron hated smoking. David walked. He had taken off the necklaces but left the copper bracelet on his arm. He flexed his arm as he walked to feel the bracelet tighten against it.

Aaron's house had a room just for music. One entire wall had shelves full of old records and tapes. Stereo components, sleek expensive ones, were stacked in a case with sliding glass doors. The lights were set into the ceiling and made the room look soft. David could feel the thickness of the carpet because he was standing in his socks. Aaron's family did not wear shoes in the house. They left them lined up by the door. David hadn't wanted to give up his shoes. One of his socks had a hole in the toe.

Aaron took an album from the shelf and slid the turntable out from the case.

"Let's start with John Coltrane. He's the best. My father heard him play once in Paris."

Aaron fiddled with the knobs on the stereo then stretched out on the carpet, ignoring the boxy black chairs. The record hissed and then the music started. Four speakers. David could feel the bass in his chest. He stood, uncertain whether he should sit in one of the chairs or stretch out next to Aaron, then decided to sit on the floor with his back against a chair.

Aaron lay with his eyes closed and his arms folded across his chest. He was smiling a little and nodding to the music. The music seemed to chase itself around and around. Horns blared and stopped. A bass came in strong and then it was gone.

"These guys are tight, aren't they?" Aaron smiled up at him. David smiled back. It wasn't like any music he had heard before. It seemed to come at him, then veer away. He wasn't sure if he liked it. Maybe it took getting used to. He pulled at the hole in his sock, trying to draw it together. The music ended and the turntable chattered as the needle lifted and swung back into its resting place.

"How about some Miles?"

"Miles?"

"Or some big band? My father just brought home a Kay Kyser that I haven't had a chance to listen to."

Big band. Guys in tuxedos in old movies.

"Miles would be great."

This music was more like a song. It wailed and drifted. It made him think of dancing.

"You know, Dave—you're the only other guy at school that listens to jazz. Everyone worships rock. Rock's okay, but it's so predictable. Do you know what I mean? With jazz, you never know when there's going to be a change-up. I love that."

David nodded. Aaron's beard was dark along his jaw line and around his lips. David wondered if he had to shave twice a day.

"We'll have to jam sometime, Dave."

David swallowed hard and nodded again. He still hadn't called Dad about the lessons. Dad had some real reasons to say no. Bad grades. That incident last summer with Kev, when they got caught breaking windows behind the mill. But that would be cover for the real reason. Which was that he didn't feel like spending his money on David.

Aaron's mother stuck her head in the door. She was wrapped in an electric blue robe and had a matching turban sort of thing on her head.

"It's getting late. David, do your parents mind that you're out so late on a school night?"

"They don't care. I mean, as long as I've done my homework."

Aaron stood and shut the door behind her. He flopped into the chair behind David.

"Wouldn't you like to go someplace where you could just listen to music all night without your parents worrying about school? I'm tired of school. Everyone talking about their cars and getting puking drunk every weekend." He reached down and rubbed David's cheek. "Shaved the old muttonchops, hey? Looks good."

The wailing music ended. Aaron's knee was resting against David's shoulder.

"Well, Dave, I have a chemistry test tomorrow. I'd better go up and look over my notes. I'll walk you up the street, though."

David stood up. His back was stiff from leaning against the chair. They put on their shoes and jackets and stepped out the door. The houses on the street were dark.

"It's really cold out here. Are you going to be all right walking home?"

"I'll be okay." They were both whispering. David found this funny and started laughing.

"You know, Dave. Sometimes I think you are crazier than anyone else I know. Without even trying."

They were walking down the street, hands in their jacket pockets, shoulders bumping in the dark. David was still laughing. He didn't think he could stop if he tried. Aaron started laughing, too. They reached the end of the road and stood together by the signpost. Aaron put his hands on David's shoulders and shook him gently, saying "crazy" over and over and laughing. David's laughing stopped as quickly as it started. He felt dizzy in the cold air and, like something tied down inside him snapped free, leaned up to kiss Aaron, a kiss in the dark that landed on the corner of his lips. Aaron dropped his hands from David's shoulders.

"Hey. Dave. I've got a girlfriend. I know I never mentioned her." David wanted to run. "We stopped going out when I moved. But we still see each other." Run and keep running. "I should have told you. She's older than me. Didn't I ever tell you?" David turned to run but Aaron grabbed his arm. His fingers dug in like the night he pulled David across the river.

"It's okay, Dave. Really."

David felt shaky and weak. He felt a cold wetness on his face. It was snowing. A normal thing. Snow. He pulled his arm away from Aaron.

"I'll get my mother's keys and drive you home. It's freezing out here."

"No. It feels good." He turned and broke into a slow jog down Route 44.

The next morning, David was in the Vice Principal's office. It was his first time. Kev was there, too, fooling with a little Christmas tree on Mr. Marshall's desk. David sat tapping on the seat of his chair, trying to swallow a bitter taste at the back of his throat. Mr. Marshall was out in the hall talking to Mr. DiPietro. All David heard was Mr. Marshall's rumbling, "I'll take care of it, Vince."

Kev had started it. But David had been waiting for the chance. Mr. DiPietro was reading *Romeo and Juliet* even though their class wasn't supposed to have Shakespeare because it was too hard. But he was reading it, even Juliet's parts. There was something about lips and hands and Kev made a kissing noise. Mr. DiPietro might have let it go but David had laughed. He decided to laugh really loud. Not just a snicker, but big choking dry-eyed laughs. Kev looked at him, slack-jawed. The other kids watched Mr. DiPietro.

Mr. DiPietro stopped and shut his book. He stood for a minute, just looking at the scene in front of him. His dark eyes were shiny and David hoped he wouldn't start crying. In a hard, tight voice he had never used on them, he told David and Kev to stand up.

"The rest of you open your workbooks."

He led them out the door and down the hall without looking to see if they followed. His thin back was stiff and straight. David was relieved. Proud of him, even.

Now Mr. Marshall walked back into the office and stood over the two boys, pounding his fist into his palm. David could hear Mr. DiPietro's shoes tapping back down the hall.

"I'd like to beat the living crap out of you two."

David wished that he would.

Still River, Winter

The worst thing was that Aaron did not seem to remember. He waited by David's locker in the afternoon. He loaned him one of his father's tapes. There was no mark on him. He was the same.

David remembered. He remembered all the time. Sometimes when he thought about it he found himself holding his hand in front of his face as though he could ward it off. At night he remembered and it was sweet. The warmth, the raspy beard. In the day, doing ordinary things, he felt sick and ashamed.

The copper bracelet sat on the dresser, where he had put it after tearing it off that night. He had twisted it, tried to break it, but it only bent. He knew he should twist it back into shape and put it back where he found it. But he did not want to touch it. Finally he flicked it off the back of the dresser and it fell down into the dust and bits of trash underneath.

Still he remembered. He looked for a sign that Aaron remembered. Sometimes he hoped he did. Sometimes he was angry that he did not, that it did not stick inside of him. It did not make him want to reach down inside and yank it out. One morning, David was combing the night snarls from his hair. He stopped, holding the comb in the air, and looked at his face in the mirror. He looked the same as before. It was not too late then. If he stopped the thoughts about Aaron—even the sweet thoughts, especially the sweet thoughts—the thing inside might stop.

That night, when Eleanor was in bed and his mother asleep on the couch, David lit a match. He singed the curly orange hairs off the back of the knuckles on his right hand.

The flame left a raised red patch on each finger. He felt better. But the next morning, everything was the same. Except that the red marks had blistered. Aaron did not notice. No one noticed.

David made himself look at Aaron. When he thought of Aaron by the river that first night, his long musician's hands, when he heard the wailing music, he made himself look. Look at the red bleeding bits of acne on Aaron's neck where he shaved in the morning. Look at his kinky hair, like a white-boy Afro, at the way he bit his fingernails. He was one of them now. He rode around with them in Mike's car, listening to the Grateful Dead, bobbing his head with the music like he liked it. All that jazz talk was for show. A new kid trying to impress. Aaron fussed about getting home in time to do his homework. He chewed breath mints before Mike dropped him off, so his parents would not smell the wine on him. They played touch football in the snow behind the school, and Aaron fell and chipped a front tooth. It gave him a goofy look, even after he had it capped.

David made himself look. After a while, the bright hum that had filled him the night he hooked the copper bracelet on his arm was gone. Sometimes he still had half-waking dreams of the wailing music, and felt Aaron's hot fingers gripping him as they crossed the river. He was not completely empty. Yet.

    The last time David saw Aaron was in the music room. It was just before Christmas. Aaron's parents were away and he was throwing a party. Mike gave David and Kev a ride. The house was hung with lights and plastic holly swags. A white wire reindeer with a red bow around its neck stood in the snow in the front yard.

    "I thought you said Aaron was Jewish," David said to Kev.

    "I dunno. My mother said Aaron's a Jewish name, that's all."

They tromped up to the door and a girl David didn't know let them in. The Stones were pounding away down the hall. He bent to take off his shoes, but Mike and Kev were already heading down the hall. He stood up and followed them into the music room. Aaron was sitting in one of the boxy black chairs wearing a Santa hat. A girl that David knew from art class was sitting on the arm of his chair. Mike pulled a bottle of peppermint schnapps from under his coat and presented it to Aaron.

"Ho ho ho!" Aaron waved at them, but he was looking up at the girl from art class. "Lotsa beer in the kitchen." His voice was slurry already.

Mike handed David a dixie cup of schnapps. He took a cool minty gulp that hit his empty stomach like a blowtorch. Mike started telling a complicated story about throwing a tie rod on the highway. Aaron was looking up at him, nodding, like he was interested. What the hell was a tie rod? Another guy came in and started throwing fake punches at Kev. David turned away and walked down the hall.

The girl who had let them in was making out with a guy in the hallway. David had to move them aside to walk past. They never looked at him. He was a ghost. He stepped outside the front door. The street was bright with Christmas lights and there were no stars. He realized that he was still holding the empty dixie cup and set it carefully on the steps. It seemed important to not throw it in the front yard. The music pounded behind him. He walked down the road and looked back, just once, to see if Aaron had followed him.

One Clean Pain

The room was cold. David sat on the edge of his bed and pulled the blanket around him. His bare feet were cold as bricks. He didn't want to lie in bed thinking anymore, but he didn't want to get up. He watched Eleanor, in her room across the hall, putting on her bulky snow boots. Her lips were pursed and she sat on the floor lacing the boots with tight even yanks. She was funny. She did everything so seriously and deliberately.

She buttoned her jacket up to her chin then pushed every wisp of hair back into her hood. It must be cold outside. Eleanor dressed for the weather. She never cared what she looked like. That would change, David thought. He smiled at her pointy hood with its grimy tassel and had an urge to get up and warn her about how — soon — it would all change. Eleanor closed her bedroom door quietly behind her then stomped down the hall.

His mother stepped out of her bedroom and stood in the hall, fumbling with the belt on her bathrobe like an old lady.

"Mom?"

"Jesus Christ! Don't jump at me like that!"

"Mom, do you think Dad would give me money for music lessons?"

"Who put that idea into your head?"

"Do you think he would?"

"If you kids were buried under an avalanche, your father wouldn't give me money for a snow shovel."

She shuffled off to the bathroom.

David dressed quickly, hating the cold damp feel of his jeans and shirt against his skin. He wondered if the furnace was out of oil again. He knew he should go downstairs to check the gauge on the tank. Be the man of the house. But it would be even colder in the basement and, if the oil tank was empty, then what?

He decided to just wrap himself in his jacket. He heard Eleanor go slamming out the back door and went out to the kitchen. The back door window was covered in frost, like big beautiful feathers. He breathed a clear circle on the glass and looked out. Eleanor was running down the street, pulling her sled behind her, eager to get to the hill on School Street. The comical hood had slid back and her hair, fine and straight like his own, was flying behind her like an orange flag. He wished he could go with her.

His shoes were beside the door, still wet from walking home the night before. He remembered how they had been damp for days after Aaron pulled him across the river. He had liked carrying around the river's wetness. That felt like a long time ago.

David thought of Aaron by the fire, that night at the river. He felt nothing. Like it had been someone else sitting there, not him, staring at Aaron's face as he talked about music. David thought of Aaron drunk and laughing in the music room, with the girl from art class leaning over him and touching his hair. Nothing. He closed his eyes and listened for the wailing music. Only the electric hum of the refrigerator.

He was David. Standing at the back door, his feet on the cold linoleum. One boy. Empty except for the thing that still stuck inside of him. One clean pain. Then he would be completely empty. Free.

David put on his jacket and wet shoes. He stepped outside into the cold. He hadn't eaten anything but he wasn't hungry. He felt hot, almost feverish in the cold air. He followed Eleanor's footprints in the snow across the yard. Where hers made a straight track up the road, he turned and headed down to the path to the river.

The Bridge

Jay Bruley stood on the stone bridge looking down into the river. The water ran heavy and fast, and did not give the ice a chance to harden. Jay had forgotten her mittens and the sleeves of her jacket were too short to bring down over her cold hands. The jacket was old. The cuffs were frayed and it was tight around her shoulders. She would need to get a new one, but she liked this one. Jay watched little needles of ice gather on the dark woolen sleeves.

She leaned her arms on the cold stones and watched the river run under the bridge. She took a penny from her jeans pocket, held it over the water, and made a wish — pleasedon'tmakeusmove. Then she tossed it into the middle of the current. She stood for a long time with tears cold on her cheeks, rubbing her chapped hands together, watching the river and the quiet banks of leafless trees.

When she saw the boy, blue-white and naked, she thought it was a huge fish. She ran to the other side of the bridge and looked to see him still carried along in the current. A boy with long, trailing hair. His hair caught on a branch in the middle of the river. The water washed around and over him.

Jay ran along the bridge, up the wooded hill, through the fields, calling Pa, calling Wes and Dale, someone to come save the boy in the river. But even as she ran, she thought of the water washing over his face. She knew the boy was past saving.

Thermal Memory

The cooling or warming effect of diurnal changes often does not reach completely down to the bottom of the snow pack. The ambient air temperature may be as much as 32 degrees higher than that of the snow. This is called *thermal memory*.

    A winter Saturday, the first day of what turned out to be a week of dreary thaw. Eleanor dragged her sled to the School Street hill. An in-between day, rain and freeze. White flakes drifted, hung, then dissolved into icy mist.

    She reached the hill and saw, with satisfaction, that the snowplows had scraped it to a hard gray slickness. Four kids stood at the top, flopped belly-down onto their sleds and slid screaming down the hill. Eleanor hurried up the edge of the street, which was piled high with big chunks of hardened snow. She could feel her heart beating when she reached the top. The other kids were pulling their sleds up again, dragging along in a line up the side of the street. She had the hill to herself. She was ready to throw her sled down and jump when someone called her name. She stood holding the sled out over the top of the hill and watched a small girl whose name she didn't know come churning across the school yard, all effort and floppy red boots. She reached Eleanor and stood red-faced, gulping air.

    "You better go home, Eleanor. There's police cars all over at your house."

Eleanor would have been embarrassed, thinking it was something ugly between her mother and father again, but the girl delivered her message kindly, without glee or excitement. Her eyes asked Eleanor not to ask questions. Eleanor tucked her sled under her arm and ran home, shortcutting through the mushy snow behind the school, leaping up and over snow banks. A mile and a half to home.

There it was all confusion. Police radios blatted like live things in the driveway. The front yard, smooth and white that morning, was trampled into muddy slush. Eleanor squeezed past bulky blue cops and neighbors caught in the midst of Saturday morning with newspapers, mixing bowls and half-eaten jelly doughnuts.

She saw her mother standing in the driveway, her old plaid coat wrapped around her and her slippers soaking up slush water. Her mouth was open and red, her voice rising loud and high like a siren, but Eleanor could not hear the words. Two policeman were standing on either side of her, looking down and scuffing their shoes in the snow. Eleanor walked towards her, through the neighbors. They touched her shoulders as she walked by, with kind words that made no sense.

"He'll be okay, sweetheart."
"They'll resuscitate..."
"You'd better not..."
"Your mother doesn't know what she's saying, hon."

Her mother turned and ran into the house, her coat flying open, showing the flowered nightgown underneath. The two cops looked up at Eleanor, then away.

It was Tina Castelli, in the third grade but still missing her two front teeth, who pulled gently on her sleeve and said, "It's your brother David, Ellie. He went under the ice in the river."

When she went in, her mother was sitting on the couch, still wrapped in the plaid coat. She was holding herself, her arms across her belly, rocking slightly back and forth.

Eleanor looked out the front window. The police were waving the neighbors out of the yard.

"Pull that curtain shut or they'll all be knocking on the door."

"What do we do?"

"Do?" Her mother looked up at her, bewildered. "What's done is done. There's nothing we can do now."

"Did he leave a note? Like people do sometimes."

Her mother gave her a sharp look. "They told you, then?"

Eleanor nodded. She sat on the edge of the couch for a while, but her mother did not say anything else. Finally, Eleanor got up and went to stand her wet boots by the back door. The phone rang and it was a boy named Aaron. He said he was a friend of David's and Eleanor was afraid, for one moment, that she was going to have to tell him what had happened. But he said he was calling with his condolences. He asked to speak to her mother, but she waved the phone away. When Eleanor hung up, after the boy said again that he was sorry, her mother told her to take the phone off the hook.

Eleanor lay on her bed through the long day, reading without making sense of the words. Her mother had turned on the television, and its sound boomed through the house. It seemed wrong, that noise, after what had happened. It made the house more empty.

Eleanor put on her jacket and stepped out into the backyard. She looked up, hoping for stars, but the sky was heavy with low clouds reflecting light from the snow. The air was thick with cold moisture and her breath made a warm fog.

They had pulled David from the river. One of the police had told her that, squatting down in the snow and looking up into her face. "You gonna be okay?" he had said and she had said yes.

They said he had done it on purpose. She could not picture that, David breaking through the ice, into the water. She could only see him carried along by the river, under the ice. That is how she liked to think of him now: still carried along, part of the river, becoming water. She looked across the yard. The pale snow seemed to glow in the night. She said David's name, once and quietly, and watched her warm breath dissolve in the cold mist.

The door opened behind her and her mother stood in the light from the kitchen.

"Come inside where it's warm." Her mother's voice was a burred whisper.

"I was thinking about David."

"You shouldn't keep thinking about him. He's in heaven now."

"I don't think so. I think he's still—"

"Never say that. God doesn't judge children. Come inside."

```
Some organisms adapt to cold climate con-
ditions through a biochemical process
called hardening. This rapid physiologi-
cal acclimatization is necessary for these
organisms to survive the winter.
```

The funeral was on Monday. It was a day like any other, a cloudy day in a week of cloudy days. A wet snow fell in the morning then changed to a thin icy drizzle by the time Eleanor and her mother arrived at the church. Her father was standing on the steps in a suit jacket, no hat or coat. He doesn't mind the cold, her mother always said. Eleanor was never sure if that meant he liked the cold or he simply did not feel it. He looked anxious, as though he had been waiting for them, but his face did not change when he walked down the steps to meet them. Eleanor could see a shiny mist of ice on his neatly combed hair. She hoped he would not spoil the day.

He turned to her first, saying, "How you doing, sweetheart?"

"I'm okay."

He stood looking down at her for a minute, shifting his shoulders under the suit jacket as though it was too tight. To her mother, he said, "We'll be sitting up front."

He took Eleanor's hand and gripped her mother's arm above the elbow. Together, they walked into the church and sat together in a front pew. Eleanor looked out the long windows and watched heavy gray clouds lumber by and the wind move through bare branches. People walked down the aisle and angled their heads to look down at them, the family.

Eleanor could hear sobs and sniffling behind her. She kept thinking the words—David is dead, my brother is dead—and waited for sadness to move through her. She watched the clouds and wondered if it was going to snow again.

The drone of the service went on. David will miss things, she thought. Icicles, snowmelt rushing down the street, cutting under big dirty March snow banks. Later, fireflies in the hedges. No. Those were things she would miss. What would David miss? His friends? The other boys, suddenly big-knuckled, their noses hardening into adult shapes. The other boys, who kept up a steady pounding on each other—fists, jokes, fuckyou. Would he miss them?

Her mother sat sobbing, hands covering her face. Her father wiped at his eyes, shamed, muttering, "Why'd he have to go and do this?"

Eleanor sat between them and tried to remember David. But she could not remember him. Only the glasses that he hated to wear, lying on the kitchen counter, the bathroom sink, left on a car seat. A black comb running through his wet hair, leaving neat even lines. A car door slamming late at night, "See you later, guys," and headlights spinning up her bedroom wall and across the ceiling. The way his hair grew in two fuzzy orange strips down the back of his neck and under his collar.

"You must miss your brother, Ellie." It was Mrs. Castelli, from down the street. She leaned over the railing and patted Eleanor's clenched fists.

Eleanor looked up into Mrs. Castelli's kind eyes, thinking, I must miss David.

When they got home, Eleanor washed the glasses and plates, rubbing the dishcloth around and around the rim of each glass, where lips touched. Her mother stood at the kitchen sink holding a carton of chocolate milk. Eleanor liked plain milk. Chocolate milk was gritty. Her mother did not drink milk at all.

"Do you want this?"

"No."

Her mother poured it down the drain.

That night her mother came into her room and sat on the edge of Eleanor's bed. Eleanor was lying under the blanket, opening and shutting a small pocketknife.

"David gave me this. He found it. It was right after Dad left. It was just what I wanted."

Her mother took the knife from her, clicked it shut and set it on the nightstand. She laid her hand on Eleanor's cheek, the way she did when Eleanor had a fever. Her hand was warm and dry.

"Try not to remember those things. It's best that way. You'll see."

```
In a process called sintering, water cre-
ated by pressure moves through the snow
pack and freezes the crystals.  This in-
creases the strength and density of the
snow pack.  This process of pressure and
```

freezing renders the snow pack impervious to further melting.

Snow fell for days. Eleanor listened to the snowplows clank and rumble late at night. Mornings, the sky was a pale even gray. The apple trees in the abandoned orchard behind the house stuck up from the snow like the claws of huge birds. The house became a place no one lived in. Frost furred the metal frames of the storm windows. Mildew grew in the corners of the kitchen ceiling.

Her mother took short-term jobs with odd hours. She came home tired, a slim brown bag with a new wine bottle cradled in the crook of her arm. Eleanor went to school and in the short afternoons took part in far-ranging and intricate snowball fights that sent her through backyards and up and over the snow-laden roofs of toolsheds. She and the other kids built bulwarks of snow blocks and crouched behind them, waiting for the other side to come by, unwary and intent on plans of its own. They dug down into the snow for stones and packed them in the middle of their snowballs. Then Brian Dunn went crying home and had to have three stitches over his right eye. Mrs. Dunn came charging over to call them wild and reckless. The other kids mumbled that they didn't mean it, but Eleanor knew Mrs. Dunn was right.

Eleanor was afraid of everything now — the river, the dogs that ran through the back yard at night, the dry hooked little seeds that she found in the folds of her wool socks — and her fear made her reckless. She took her sled to the School Street hill and stayed there until the streetlights came on, the stars came out, the other kids all went home. The metal runners on her sled struck sparks on bits of bare asphalt. At the bottom of the hill, she would skid her sled sideways toward the traffic. Belly down, her legs spread out and her toes gouging the ice, she taunted the drivers. Go ahead, run me over. When they swerved and looked down at her with their mouths gaping open, she felt a wild power. A tire sliding by her head or touching the tip of her tongue to hot oatmeal. Or her mother's eyes coming into focus on her, the one who was left. It was useless to try to avoid danger. It was everywhere.

One morning, a rare morning that caught them together, Eleanor looked at her mother across the kitchen table. Her mother was shuffling bills and receipts. Her cigarette smoldered in the ashtray at her elbow and the hand that reached for it was bony like a bat's wing. The knuckles stood out sharply along the fingers, the tendons stretched tight under the skin. The hand lifted the cigarette to pale lips that tightened around it like a drawstring purse. A sleeve slid back from a bony wrist. Nothing but skin and bones. That was her mother's phrase. Nothing but skin and bones. When had she last seen her mother eat? A sandwich, wrapped up "for later." A can of soup opened and left on the counter. Crackers broken on a plate.

Eleanor began to watch her mother. One night, she got up when her mother came home from work and made her a fried egg sandwich. She set the plate in front of her, watched her pick up the sandwich and held her breath, waiting for her mother to eat, to chew and swallow. She did not dare to move, to break this wished-for chain of events.

"I'm sorry. I'm just too tired to eat."

She tried other things. Hot corn bread from a mix, Rice Krispy squares, applesauce with cinnamon.

Her mother smiled up at her, pushed the food around on the plate, then covered it with foil. Through the winter, the refrigerator was full of plates and bowls with ragged bits of foil over them.

"That was sweet of you, but I'm not hungry tonight."

"You eat these. Bring some to school for your friends."

And one night: "I'm trying, Ellie. I really am."

When March came, the bulwarks of snow that crisscrossed the backyards melted and tumbled in on themselves. Out in the orchard, the concave tunnels of field mice lay open and exposed by the melting snow.

Eleanor came in from the orchard to the cardboard smell of take-out hamburgers. Her mother sat at the kitchen table folding back the wrapper on a soft thin burger. She bit down on the burger, chewed, swallowed, bit again. Licked mustard off her finger. She looked up at Eleanor, who stood staring in the doorway. She pushed a bag across the table toward her.

"I saved one for you. They were having a sale. Two for one."

By April, the sharpness of her cheekbones had softened. But she was always thin after that.

The Riverine Environment

The edge of a wilderness habitat is often the most important ecologically in that it supports a diversity of wildlife not found in the interior. The interface of two "edges" — for example, the aquatic and terrestrial habitats of the riverine environment — is called an *ecotone*.

Early morning. The river is slow and golden at the end of a dry summer. Eleanor is fourteen now. Sometimes she thinks it is strange that she loves this place. But she can remember here. At the river, she is by herself, but not alone.

She knows the names of everything.

Whirlagig beetles, gathering and scattering across the calm shallows. Horsetail rushes with their ancient jointed stalks, living witnesses to that first crawl from water to land. Dragonflies, damselflies. Spring azure butterflies, pale silver-blue by summer's end.

The sudden red flash of a swamp maple. The precise delicate paw print of a river otter. Bank swallow nests like empty little caves. Husks of caddisfly larva cases drifting on the bottom. Red-tinged curls of paper birch bark. The hand-shaped leaves of sweet-rooted sassafras. Granite veined with mica and quartz.

Bloodroot, stonefly, spicebush, sweetgum, cinnamon fern, jewelweed, false Solomon's seal. Pickerel, pike, early meadow rue, poison ivy, Canada mayapple, wild sarsaparilla, pseudoscorpions, daddy longlegs, hophornbeam. Maidenhair fern, interrupted fern, wild ginger, tamarack.

Red-backed salamanders, fox grapes, red-eyed vireo, northern waterthrush, northern watersnake, red-shouldered hawk.

Leafhoppers, treehoppers, kadydids, cicadas.
Goldthread with its healing root.
Butternuts that stain the fingers.
Devil's bit or fairy wand.
November-blooming witch-hazel.
Eleanor knew them all.
Near the other shore, someone floating. And she thought, for just one moment... No. No, of course not.

The Swimming Place

The swimming place was wide and deep, even in late summer. Years ago, Jay had watched Wes climb high in a willow that over-hung the bank to tie a rope to a thick branch so they could swing down to the water. Wes could hold himself up straight on the rope and skim his feet across the surface of the water, sending out a fan of spray. Someone, since then, had added an old tire to the rope and most people considered that an improvement. But Jay had liked gripping the end of the plain rope and trying to hold her feet just right so they skimmed over the water to make a rooster tail.

On weekends, the swimming place was noisy with older boys and girls and their babies and toddlers. The girls sat on blankets and kept an eye on their kids splashing and squabbling in the shallows. The boys swung on the rope and yodeled. They brought radios and coolers of beer. Sometimes Wes and Dale knew them and would sit on the edge of a blanket and drink a bottle of beer. No one ever offered one to Jay.

The tree with the rope had a BB-pocked sign that said Private-No Swimming. By most summer Sunday afternoons, the owners of the river bank, tired of rock 'n' roll and drunken Tarzan yells, would call the police. The police would drive up, saunter down the bank, sweating in long pants and tight shoes, and jerk their thumbs towards the sign. The underage girls would slip beer bottles back into coolers and grab their babies out of the river, while their boyfriends hauled diaper bags and radios up the riverbank to the road.

But it was mid-week, still early morning and getting close to fall, so Jay had the swimming place to herself. She walked along the bank until she found a sun-warm rock and sat there for a while, watching blue darning needles land and lift, snatching invisible things out of the air. Jay sat with her legs drawn up, her chin resting on her knees. The sun beat down on her black hair, bristly with a new haircut. She ran her hand through it and it was hot to the scalp. In the calm shallows, shiny black water beetles circled and circled and she wondered how she had suddenly gone from too young to too old.

She had always chased after Wes and Dale, to go fishing or sleeping out nights, their exciting plans. You're too little, they said, and Pa always agreed. She stomped on the porch until the floorboards jumped and old Charley had to leave his spot by the door. Then Pa would put his hands on her shoulders and steer her into the house saying, "When you get a little older..."

Now she was fourteen. That morning, as she followed Wes and Dale from room to room watching them gather up fishing gear and pack egg sandwiches, Pa had looked up from his coffee and said, "You're too old now to be chasing after your brothers."

When Jay pointed out that she had caulked the very canoe that Wes and Dale were loading onto the van, Pa had suggested that she spend the day with Auntie Pauline.

"She said to come over and she'd fix your hair up pretty."

Jay tossed a pebble into the circling water beetles and they scattered. In another minute, they were circling again and she was hot enough to get into the water. She stripped down to her bathing suit, tugged at the too-tight straps and waded in. Her feet on the gravel bottom looked golden in the oak-steeped water. She bent forward, dove, and blew out a stream of bubbles that trailed softly up her cheek. She hung for a moment on the bottom, beating her hands against the water to stay under. The deep water was cold. Sunlight angled down and glinted off bits of mica in the gravel. The only sound was the steady thrum of water pressing against her eardrums. Jay arched her back and rose, breaking the surface and breathing deeply. Everything looked bright and sharp-edged—the black tire on its rope, blue sky and green leaves, her clothes in a red heap on the bank. Jay rolled over on her back and floated outstretched in the slow current.

She sensed before she saw that someone else was on the opposite shore. A girl standing ankle-deep in the river, bent at the waist, looking down into the water. Jay turned her head and watched her. She was skinny and her legs were too long for her shorts. Her hair was carrot-orange and tied back in a lop-sided ponytail. She was wearing a sleeveless jersey, and even from across the river, Jay could see two bright spots of sunburn on her shoulders. She was holding a magnifying glass in one hand and a book in the other. Her sneakers hung around her neck and swung forward every time she bent down to look at something with the magnifying glass.

Jay closed her eyes and floated, looking at the red sun through her eyelids. She wanted to stay there, floating, knowing the girl with the magnifying glass, the river detective, was wading on the other shore. When she opened her eyes, the girl was gone. A kingfisher flew from a willow branch, feathers wet and sparkly in the sun, and she was by herself again.

Cedar Waxwings

On the morning of Eleanor's first day of high school, she stood in front of the bathroom mirror. She sniffed the sleeve of her shirt, the sweet chemical smell of the store. Brand new, a crease denting the front from being folded in its cellophane bag. A blue shirt to match her eyes. She looked at herself in the mirror. Her ordinary blue eyes. Straight fine eyebrows. Clear skin. A few freckles across her nose that would fade by October, maybe. Neck a little long and thin. Button? Unbutton? Hair tucked behind her ears? No. If she gathered her hair back, let the sides hang loose, loop over her ears. Loop. Okay. Pretty? Okay.

On the bus, she found an empty seat, then Dennis Kibby sat next to her. It wasn't true that he smelled, he smelled like everyone else, no matter what the kids said at her old school. In high school, no one would know the names they called him. There would be eleven hundred kids at the high school. That's what the newpaper said. Record Enrollment Means Overcrowding.

"Are you sure they're letting kids wear jeans to school now?" her mother had asked at the door that morning.

"Everyone else wears them."

"Fix your collar. That's better. Now you look just like everyone else."

Eleanor looked out the window of the bus while it waited in a long line of buses in the asphalt circle in front of the school. The high school was a low flat-roofed building made of yellow bricks. Hundreds of kids milled around outside — running and dodging through the crowd, waving and yelling, weaving in and out and through like bees in a hive. Finally, Eleanor's bus rolled into place and the door opened. She stepped down into the huge crowd, looking around at all the kids, feeling excited and hopeful. A white paper airplane sailed up on a breeze against the September blue sky. The heavy summer heat was gone.

Eleanor licked her finger and held it out in the breeze. East, likely to bring new weather.

"Whatcha pointing at?" Two girls stood in front of her. Stacy and Carole Anne from her old school. She shoved her hands in her jeans pockets and they dove back into the crowd, shoulder to shoulder and giggling.

The day went by in confusion. The halls were narrow and dark and jammed with kids. It was hard to find the classrooms, especially the temporary classrooms in offices and storage rooms. Those rooms had stenciled paper signs—T1, T2—taped to their doors and the older kids tore them down. The biology lab, a real laboratory with long black-topped tables, had so many kids in it that Eleanor had to sit in the back on the edge of a sink.

At lunch, in the huge glare of the cafeteria, she stood with her tray and hoped that someone would wave her to a seat. Before everyone saw that she belonged nowhere, she sat down at a table full of older girls. They flicked raisins at each other all through lunch. She pretended to read her biology book.

By the time the buzzer sounded for the last class, Eleanor was tired. She had lost a new pen and had a scrape on her elbow. Someone had shoved her against a locker, probably just by accident. The kids had already started to separate into groups of fours and fives. Clumps of kids blocked the halls and doorways. They fanned out into classrooms then were drawn back together when the buzzer sounded. They reminded Eleanor of the way metal filings bunched into bristly clumps with the wave of a magnetic wand.

Her last class was Western Civilization. She was relieved to find the room quickly. It was nearly empty and she was able to claim a seat in the back next to the window. Late kids had to take the front seats. The teacher, Mrs. Langevin, did not welcome them to their first day. When the 2:30 buzzer sounded, she handed each of them a heavy book, then made them call out their names for attendance. A boy she didn't know said his name was Bowzer Noonan. Mrs. Langevin corrected him—"Gerard Noonan"—without looking up from the attendance list. Bowzer looked around the room and grinned. When no one even smiled, he looked down and quietly gouged at his desk with a pencil.

Mrs. Langevin began with the first city, the city of Ur, and the Fertile Crescent, the Cradle of Civilization. She chalked an outline on the board with a Roman numeral heading each section. I. Cities.

A girl opened the door and stepped inside. She had to walk across the front of the room to the last empty seat, the front seat by the window. She pulled a notebook and pencil out of an ugly burlap tote bag and sat, ready. Mrs. Langevin looked at the clock then at the girl.

"Don't expect to come and go as you please in this classroom."

The girl looked back at her, with her pencil still poised for notes.

"Jeanette Bruley is the only name that I have not checked off on my roster. I presume that is you."

"Jay Bruley."

She looked like a jay, Eleanor thought, like a bluejay. The way her straight black hair grew thick on the top of her head. She had something of their boldness, too. Her clothes were all wrong—a rust-colored jacket with big buttons, cheap jeans with white stitching, the horrid burlap tote bag. But she didn't seem to notice. Her hair was cut bluntly below her ears as though someone had cut it off as punishment. But she did not look like she would let anyone do that. And she did not look like she belonged to people who would inflict such a haircut. Jay Bruley.

Mrs. Langevin crossed her arms and looked down at the girl. Bowzer Noonan was grinning again. Then Mrs. Langevin turned back to the chalkboard. II. The Rise of Commerce.

Outside the window, the leaves on the top branches of the oaks had a faint reddish color they had not had the week before. Whoever had cut the strip of lawn between the school and the trees had left the clippings in dry rows like a miniature hay field. A pin cherry sapling had grown up by the window, too close to the building to be clipped by the mower. It was spindly, but full of small black fruits.

A flock of cedar waxwings descended on the pin cherry like they'd been shaken down from the sky. They were sleek-feathered, warm yellow-brown. The bright red tips on their wing feathers did look like candle wax, Eleanor thought. They called to each other with high airy whistles and ate the pin cherries. Eleanor heard the rustling of leaves and the occasional snap of a berry pulled from its stem.

"...and the confluence of these rivers became a center of commerce and culture..."

Down the row of seats, the girl called Jay was also staring out the window at the waxwings in the pin cherry tree. She turned her head back a little, caught Eleanor's eye, and smiled.

"Can you repeat for the class, Miss Bruley, the names of those two rivers?"

Jay looked down at her desk, but it was clear that she wouldn't find the answer there. Everyone stared.

Eleanor snapped her head back to the window and stared resolutely at the waxwings, who were still gobbling berries. She felt, rather than saw, the husky boy in the seat next to her turn to see what she was looking at. The girl in front of her also turned to look. Then Bowzer Noonan. Then Neil Shaugnessy, a boy she knew from her old school. Then a quiet girl, who had sat in the front row by choice. Then Mrs. Langevin.

"Well, it looks like those sparrows have caught everyone's attention, but I can assure you that the Tigris and the Euphrates will be on this Friday's quiz." She turned back to the chalkboard. IV. Travel and Trade.

Jay looked out the window again. Eleanor realized that the cedar waxwings had flown. They had not left a single berry.

Eleanor thought about Jay on the bus ride home and while she made a dinner of pancakes and cut book covers out of paper bags. She thought of them watching cedar waxwings while pin cherries shook loose to the ground. She was standing alone in a field, watching a hawk circle, and suddenly Jay was beside her, pointing. Look.

I know where the herons nest at the river.

I know where there's a hollow tree that you can stand inside of and look up at the sky.

I know how to find the Big Dipper.

I can find the North Star.

Do you know why beech trees grow in circles?

They were wading in the river. Look, Jay. Look at this.

She stood in front of the bathroom mirror, loosening the rubber band in her hair, letting her hair fall out of its carefully casual loops. Wispy red hair. Jay's hair was thick and dark, like the pelt of an animal. An otter. She ran her finger across her eyebrows so they were straight and smooth. She caught her smile in the mirror. David. Standing in front of the mirror one morning. Slicking back his hair with a wet comb. His wet hair looked dark and shiny. Neat lines from the comb. He had caught her watching and said, "I think I'm supposed to have black hair. Don't you think so?" He smiled at her. Not a grin. A sad secret smile. He's trying this out on me, Eleanor remembered thinking. He's practicing this smile for someone else.

She lay in bed and tried to stop thinking about Jay, fell asleep promising that she would not look for her at school tomorrow.

The Out-of-Season Deer

Jay opened her eyes to gray sky and one bright planet rippling in the thick glass of the windowpane. She wanted to go back to sleep and closed her eyes. She wanted to dream about the red-haired girl at school, the river detective. They sat together at lunch sometimes, but they did not talk. Eleanor—that was her name—read a book. Jay ate quickly. What was there to say?

She opened her eyes again, got up and stepped out into the hall in her bare feet. The door to Wes and Dale's room was open but the room was dark. She heard them talking downstairs and Wes's excited laugh. Then she remembered. They were going hunting this morning.

Yesterday, Pete Slater had told Wes that he'd seen a buck with a full rack down in the swamp that stood within his property lines. He said that Wes and Dale were welcome to use his deer-stand in the swamp in case the buck came by again. Hunting season on deer wasn't open yet, but Slater figured a man could do what he wanted on his own land. Pa had come home and found Wes and Dale cleaning and oiling the old rifles in the parlor.

"I hope that when morning comes, you boys will show better judgment."

Jay knew there had been a time when he would have taken the rifles from their hands, put them back in the gun case and closed the glass door gently. Pa let things go now. He hadn't mowed their field since the surveyors sighted through it to estimate water levels. Now the field was full of runty cedar and birch and woodchuck holes. Jay had watched him hang his jacket on the hook by the door and scrub his hands at the kitchen sink. In the parlor, Wes and

Dale slid rifle bolts back and forth, a smooth sound, like steady rain.

Pa had always said there was something wrong about hunting out-of-season, something that had nothing to do with getting caught by a game warden. Although the fines were steep and a lot of the new people moving in didn't think that hunting had a place in their woods. Most of the new people posted their land to keep it off-limits to hunters and trespassers. Old Slater was one of the few that valued his land for its pasturage and well-drained soil rather than its seclusion. But hunting out-of-season had nothing to do with laws or boundaries.

At the end of each deer season, whether he had been out in the woods or not, their father would say, "Well, they can rest now." Jay knew the deer didn't have a calendar to mark the dates, but she imagined that when they heard that first shot they got scared. And they stayed scared until the woods had been quiet for a long time. Jay had seen the tired, drag-footed way Pa climbed the stairs to his room. This year the deer would have a few extra weeks of fear.

Jay walked downstairs in her bare feet. The gun case in the parlor was empty. Wes and Dale let the back door slam and revved the engine of the van to get it warmed up faster. Then Jay heard the van going through the gears up the road.

She stood in the kitchen and shut her eyes, picturing Slater's swamp, the maples all October fire. She saw the buck stepping through the red leaves in black mud, bending to browse the twigs on the red-osier dogwood. She willed him to run. But each time she shut her eyes he was still there, bending his head low. His antlers spread in a graceful arc and the brown fur on his neck caught the early morning sun. Jay heard her father stirring upstairs and spooned coffee into the enamel pot.

Jay thought of the deer all day, and when she got home that night, it was already dark and cold. A heavy dew had fallen at sunset and everything lay under a slick shine. The van was in the yard and Jay made herself walk to the backyard to see if the carcass of the buck was hanging from the horse-chestnut tree. It wasn't. She smiled for the first time all day. The light was on in the kitchen and she could see Dale and Wes sitting at the table. Pa was standing at the head of the table, his head bent as though listening. When she opened the door, they all jumped and looked at her like rabbits caught in the garden.

"You see what you've done," Pa said to the boys. "Now we will be afraid of every sound we hear." Wes and Dale looked away from him.

"What happened?" Jay asked. The boys looked at each other, then up at Pa.

"Tell her. It's not my story to tell."

They had driven through Slater's gate before sunrise and left the van in his cornfield, which was still littered with fallen and broken stalks. Slater had told Wes that the deer-stand was in the only tall pine tree in the whole swamp. They found it easily, a few boards nailed onto two sturdy branches, just big enough for the two of them. The stand was only eight feet off the ground but gave a good view of a small patch of bog with a clear spring-fed pool. Slater's dog had startled the buck at this pool only the day before. A pattern of tracks, both dry and fresh, said that the buck had been drinking at the pool for some time.

Wes and Dale climbed up onto the platform and settled in. Dale sat with his back against the trunk and sipped coffee from a thermos, his rifle across his lap. Wes crouched at the edge of the platform, feeling for the wind direction.

"If he keeps coming down that path like he's been coming, we'll be crosswind to him. We'll have to be awful quick."

"I wouldn't sit at the edge like that with your safety off. You fall off of this stand, you're liable to blow your head off."

The sun was well up by now, shining sideways through the branches and flashing on the red maple leaves. A grouse strutted by beneath them, making a tick-tick sound like a tiny hammer on wood. Wes raised his gun and aimed, then grinned back at Dale.

"Shoot that bird and that's the last thing we'll see all day," Dale said.

They got restless after a while. When the sun reached the bare tops of the trees, Dale whispered that they should get back to the van and head for work. Wes nodded, but they both sat there, held by the warm sunlight and the fiery beauty of the swamp—the scarlet maples, gold viburnums, a speckled alder bent under the glorious orange weight of a bittersweet vine.

When they became aware of the buck, he was standing by the spring. He was not high at the shoulder, but his rack was large and graceful, the antlers curving up as though weightless. The buck was so close that they could see his black leathery nose twitching in the still air. Neither boy moved. A slight breeze stirred the hair at the back of their necks. That was enough. The buck caught their scent and snapped his head around. In one bound he was back in the woods. The leaves closed behind him. Wes jumped up, yelled "Goddamn!" and fired into the woods where the deer had been. The sound of the shot rang in the air.

Dale turned on him. "That was stupid. What did you do that for?"

"If you don't shoot at something, you ain't been hunting. You've just been sitting on your ass up in a tree all morning."

They climbed down out of the deer stand and stood stretching their cramped muscles. Dale bent down and touched a finger to a leaf on a red-osier dogwood. He held out the finger to Wes. It was streaked with blood.

"I think you must of nicked him."

"Nicked him? Look at all that blood in there. I'd say I hit him pretty square on."

"Then we need to find him."

"We can't go chasing an out-of-season deer all over the county, Dale. We got to get to work anyway."

Dale turned away from him and parted the blood-splattered branches. He stepped into the woods and the branches closed behind him. Wes stood for a minute banging the stock of his rifle against the ground. Then he tucked the gun under his arm and followed.

The deer had left an even trail of blood through the dogwoods and alders and up a rise where the woods opened out and the ground was hard underfoot. The trail of blood drops and sticky fur followed a dry stream bed, made a straight line across a dirt road, and then headed down into another swampy piece of land. The sun was high and both boys were sweating.

They came to a low stone wall that bordered a close-clipped green lawn. The lawn rolled up to a big house with rows of windows and skylights. Drops of blood glinted in the green grass. The boys stood wiping sweat off their faces, reluctant to step out into the open.

"Get off my property."

They had been so intent on the small details that they hadn't seen her. She was standing by the wall in the shadow of an oak. She was thin, silver-haired, wearing a green jacket and expensive leather and rubber boots. Hunter's boots, had she known it. She had never seen a gun up close before and she was scared. She looked down at the bloody grass and back at the boys. They would not meet her eyes.

"My land is posted. From that road back there all the way to the river. Take your guns and get out." Dale could hear the fear shaking in her voice and it made him feel worse, that she would think he was a man capable of hurting her. He and Wes headed back into the woods. They had walked a few steps when they heard her again.

"You couldn't even give him a quick merciful death, could you?"

The next morning, Jay left the house at sunrise. She cut through the woods up to Slater's pasture, then followed the cow-track to the cornfield. It still had tire marks from the van pressed into the soft dirt. She found the deer-stand in the one tall pine and the spring beneath it. The small green leaves on the ground around the spring were scattered with dark red drops. She bent to touch one. They were wild cranberries. The night's heavy dew had cleansed the woods of the deer's blood.

It was a hot day for October, muggy and close. She pushed on through the woods wiping sweat and the webs of caterpillars off her face. She came out on the dirt road and saw Dale's bootprint on the other side. She stepped quietly past the POSTED signs nailed to the trees at twelve-foot intervals. She stopped to listen and heard only a dog barking in the distance.

Jay trespassed all the time. Signs were all over the woods and she never paid attention to them. She had never felt that those signs were for her. She was usually taking a short-cut or looking for a flicker nest, or just walking to think by herself for a while. But her brothers wounding an out-of-season deer made her feel akin to people who came to the woods to do damage or do things they wouldn't do in town.

Jay had a knife, a piece of soft flannel, tape and a bottle of antibiotics in her pockets. If she found the deer laying-up in a thicket, exhausted and drained, she would dig out the bullet. Then she would put antibiotics in the wound and bind it up. She had helped her father do that, years ago, when a hunter had shot one of their dogs. If she found the deer near death, in pain but still breathing, she would take the knife and slit his throat.

Jay came to the wall, the well-kept yard and the woman's house. She skirted the yard keeping well in the woods. On the other side of the yard, a rusted piece of barbed wire fence was twisted into the wall. On one of the barbs, she found a tuft of brown fur. She walked a straight line from that fur down a wooded slope to the river.

She stood on the river bank with the POSTED signs behind her. She was hot. Tiny flies buzzed around her ears. She scanned the ground for deer sign but there was nothing. A big fallen willow blocked the path going upriver. The water was high for mid-October and flowing with heavy force. Jay turned right and walked downstream. She was tired. She was almost forgetting why she was out in the woods. The river kept up a steady murmur.

She found the buck at a bend in the river, where it swept around into wide shallows. The buck lay with his head twisted over his shoulder as though he had died looking back in fear. Flies buzzed around his eyes. Jay could see a small dark hole in his side matted with black blood. Her brother had shot him through the ribs. A lung shot.

Jay put her hands in her pockets and touched the knife and her other mercy supplies. She squatted down by the deer and rubbed the soft whorls of fur at the base of his antlers. She wanted to do something before she left him. Say something that would pay homage and ask forgiveness. She tried to remember what was said at her mother's grave, but she had been young then and the words had rolled over her without meaning. So she whispered the only prayer she knew, the Grace that her father said before their meals: "We ask your blessing, Lord, on these fruits of your bounty and on those of us gathered here. We trust in Your mercy and grace." The last line she addressed directly to the deer. Then she knelt beside the shallows and washed her hands in the river.

When Jay got back to the house, it was nearly dark. A breeze had picked up and the air had gone cool and dry. The light was on in the barn, and Wes was crouched down just inside the open door. He was holding something in his hands and looked up smiling as Jay walked towards him.

"What have you got?"

"Black racer." Wes held the slim head of a glossy black snake between his thumb and forefinger. With his other hand, he cradled the loose coils of its body.

"He's big. Where did you find him?"

"Over in that corner. I think he's planning to spend the winter in here." Wes stood and held the snake up to the light. "Beautiful, isn't he?"

"You going to keep him?"

"No use keeping a snake. They never take to you. They don't even see you. Look at this one. He knows something's got him pinned down, but he doesn't even know it's me." He gently set the snake back down on the barn floor. It glided off to the corner in the long straight way of racers. Wes watched it then turned to head back into the house.

"Wes. I found the deer."

He stopped and stood with his arms folded.

"I thought you might want to know. He's okay now. He's dead." Jay remembered the deer's head twisted over his shoulder, the deep hole in the soft fur. She would not tell all that to Wes.

"Well of course he's dead. What did you expect?" Wes reached to switch off the light.

"You hit him in the side. The lungs. Stomach maybe."

"Don't tell Pa that." He looked down at Jay as if to see if he needed to say more. She pulled back her lips in a smile.

"How long do you think that racer is, Wes?"

75

"Next time I'll bring out a yardstick for you." He switched off the light and stepped out of the barn. "And thanks. For letting me know about...what you found." He walked up to the house.

Jay stayed outside. Her shirt was still damp with sweat and the wind chilled it against her skin. She was tired. The lightness she had felt walking back from the river was gone. The deer had become a burden again. A story she could not tell.

The Hawk

Route 14, the road to the country part of town, was lined with oak trees still green in late October. Eleanor watched out the window for breaks in the trees where fields were full of bright yellow light and cows. There were only four kids left on the bus. Eleanor, Jay, and the Vickery twins, who were poking at their eyes with mascara brushes as the bus bumped along. The bus stopped at a rural mailbox on a post and Jay tapped her hand.

"This is my stop." Eleanor and Jay jumped down off the bus. The Vickerys didn't look up from their mirrors and the driver just said, "Careful now," and snapped the door behind them. Jay pulled the mail out of the box and they walked down a gravel road crowded with goldenrod and fall asters.

"Do you have cows?"

"No. We used to. Everyone did. But I hardly remember them. It was a long time ago, before I was even in school."

The house was back from the road. Gravel mixed into the weeds in the front yard. Two junk cars leaned on broken axles and a mail truck was up on cinder blocks. A dark blue pickup still had its tires, but the paint had gone milky on the fenders. Jay's house was three houses pushed up against each other, like the Bruleys added whatever came along. The back end of a trailer was attached to one side and an unpainted shed to the other. The shed had one blue-framed window. The main house sat in the middle with a steep-pitched roof and a porch. White paint was chipping off its clapboards in tiny neat squares. Eleanor was glad it would be dark by the time her mother came to pick her up.

Her mother had strong opinions about shabby houses and the people who lived in them.

A huge collie rose and stiff-legged his way down the porch steps. He rolled his narrow face against Jay's thigh.

"This is Charley. He's twelve and can't see a thing anymore." Jay scratched the thin dry fur down the middle of his back and he wriggled his shoulders. They walked up the worn granite steps. Charley struggled back up the steps and eased himself down onto a pile of braided rugs.

The door was unlocked but the house was quiet and empty. The rooms were clean and spare with wide floorboards painted white. There was a real woodstove, a galvanized pail full of kindling and two wooden rockers. In one corner, there was a glass gun case framed in dark wood. Inside were two rifles, old complicated-looking things resting against carved pegs. A tall bookcase stood in the opposite corner, all the spines lined up neatly.

A shelf ran high along the back wall with only two things on it. One was a rough-carved wooden duck painted black and white with a golden glass eye. The duck seemed to be swimming toward a photograph in a metal frame. It was a black and white snapshot of a woman with heavy lipstick and light hair curled carefully around her face. She was wearing a plaid coat and at her feet was a large fish. She had fine features and blond hair. But the set of her shoulders and the way her eyes stared straight at whoever was holding the camera looked like Jay.

"Is that your mother?" Eleanor hadn't meant to ask. It slipped out. She looked at Jay, hoped she wouldn't cry. It was the saddest thing — wasn't it? — to have your mother die.

"Yeah. They were ice-fishing up at my uncle's place when they took that picture. That fish weighed twelve pounds." The fish.

Jay led her into the kitchen. It had a big gas range with brass fittings, a curtainless window, a well-scrubbed sink and orderly shelves. A long wooden table flanked by low benches held down the other end of the room. On it was one breach of discipline—a knife and a scattering of crumbs.

Jay poured two cups of cider from a jug without a stopper. Eleanor drank. The cider was thick and tart, not like store cider. She looked out the back window where the yard rolled down to a gone-wild vegetable patch. Someone had piled dry corn stalks into a heap.

"Finish up. I want to show you something." Eleanor tilted her head back to get the last pulpy dregs. Jay rinsed the cups in the deep sink and they waded across the yard through ankle-high blown dandelions to a sway-backed shed. Against one wall was a hutch with gleaming chicken wire stapled to a wooden frame. As they approached, something inside the hutch shifted and gave a high mewling call. Jay ran ahead.

"Look. A hawk. My brother Wes brought her home day before yesterday. Flew right into his windshield. Must have been going after something and got confused."

"Is she hurt?"

"No. She was just knocked out for a minute. At least, that's what Wes says. He's going to train her to hunt. Like those old-time falconers."

"How do you know she's a she?"

"That's what Wes says."

Wes had nailed a dead branch inside the cage as a perch, but the hawk was not sitting on it. She was huddled on the wire mesh floor in a corner. She was beautiful. Cocoa-brown feathers riffled thick and soft down her back to a ginger-red wedge of a tail. From her throat to her feathery legs, she was the color of cream. She watched the two of them steadily, blinking once, quickly. Then her eyes were on them again. Her dangerous beak was gaping open, like she was dumbfounded or trying to catch her breath.

A van pulled into the yard and two older boys got out. Dale and Wes. Dale looked like Jay, neatly built, with dark hair hanging over his eyes in a thick wedge. Wes was taller, sharp-angled and pale, with straw-colored hair pulled back in a ponytail. Both wore paint-splattered jeans and workshirts, the sleeves rolled tight over their forearms. Wes jogged down to the cage. Dale trailed behind and stopped a few paces away.

"She finally calm down?"

"Yeah. She's just kind of mopey now. I was showing her to Eleanor." Wes peered into the cage.

"She's not using my perch."

"Maybe she's hungry." Dale said it quietly but he sounded so fierce that Jay and Eleanor turned to look at him. He was standing on the slope of the hill, toeing at the ground, his hands jammed into his pockets. Wes didn't turn.

"The hungrier she gets, Dale, the faster she'll learn." He pulled a pair of stiff work gloves out of his back pocket and pulled them on. He lifted the latch on the cage. Dale turned and walked back up to the house. Wes opened the door slowly. The hawk, instead of bolting for the opening, shrank against the back of the cage and beat her wings. They stretched wider than the cage and struck the sides. The coppery flight feathers caught and bent in the chicken wire. There was the soft whump of the wings and the clatter of talons on metal. Wes put one hand into the cage and moved it steadily toward the bird. She looked down at it and Eleanor waited for her to use the fierce beak. Wes quickly closed his hand around her feet. She fought then. She stabbed at the glove and his bare arm, drawing blood once along the blue veins of his inner arm. He swung the door wide open and drew her out. She was flapping and straining, as though she would pull him into the sky. Eleanor watched his hand, willed the glove to loosen its hold. Wes thrust the hawk back into the cage, slammed the door, and latched it.

"She's still not ready for lessons. Not by a long shot." He licked at his bleeding arm. The hawk was standing at the bottom of the cage, wings open and drooping, head down. Eleanor looked away. Jay's mouth was clamped shut. Wes pulled off the gloves and held a hand out to Eleanor.

"We never got introduced. I'm Wes." She put her hand in his then pulled it away. His arm was still bleeding. He grinned.

"Have Jay show you the rabbits. You'll like them. They're cute." He walked back to the van. Jay shrugged and wordlessly led her behind the shed. There was another wood and chicken wire cage. There was straw at the bottom of this one, and curled in it were six tawny rabbits. Babies. Their tiny ears, like moth wings, laid back close against their heads.

"They probably aren't more than a week or two old. Dale found them up in Slater's field before they mowed. They were just curled up pink things then. He carried them home in his jacket pocket. Looked like an owl got the mother. There were bits of fur all over the place."

One nosed its way over to the side of the hutch and pushed its face through the wire. It had short fine whiskers already. Eleanor reached out to stroke the silky brown fur along its nose and it twisted its head up to give her finger a sharp nip.

"What are you going to do with them when they grow up?"

Jay looked back toward the hawk cage. "I don't know. They can't be pets, you know. They're born wild."

"What about the hawk? She was born wild."

Jay's mouth twisted, then settled into a stubborn line. "Wes isn't making a pet out of that hawk. And if you don't think he can tame her, you don't know my brother. He's got the gift. He used to have a weasel that would take meat from his hand. He's going to teach me, too."

They walked back up to the house. Wes was pulling ladders out of the back of the van. He picked one up, balanced it on his shoulder and strolled over to the open door of a weed-choked barn. He walked straight and graceful. Dale was nowhere in sight.

"I need to start fixing supper before Pa gets home."

Eleanor followed Jay into the kitchen and sat on one of the benches. Jay took potatoes out of a bin under the counter and started scrubbing them in the sink. She was hunched over and kept looking back, self-consciously, at Eleanor.

"Do you like to cook?" Eleanor asked.

"Nope."

"I can help peel those."

"I'm used to doing it myself." Jay banged a drawer shut and started chopping at the potatoes, peels and all.

"Maybe I'll go outside until dinner's ready."

Jay looked relieved. Eleanor went out the back door and walked through the yard whacking the heads off dandelions and sending their seed-kites into the air. Her eyes were half-closed and she turned herself away from the shed and the caged hawk. She slashed at the dandelions until the air was full of seed-kites. A whippoorwill started its frantic wheep-a-wee. The sun was throwing spears of light through the oaks. She opened her eyes. She was in front of the cage. The hawk was still sitting in the middle of it. She had pulled in her wings, but one was hitched higher than the other. It didn't seem to fit against her body. Across the light feathers on her chest there was a streak of blood. Eleanor hoped it belonged to Wes.

The latch was jerry-rigged, a bent nail dropped down through a piece of a door hinge. Eleanor reached carefully toward the latch, looking from the hawk, to the yard where Wes was wrestling with a tire, back to the latch. The hawk lunged and she stifled a scream into a low grunt. The hawk threw herself at the door again. As she opened her wings, Eleanor saw blood clotted in the soft feathers at the front edge of one wing, where the skin stretched tightly over the bone. A shape stepped out from the side of the shed. She jumped.

"There you are." Her mother stepped forward. "It's a good thing I decided to look for this place before dark. It's in the back of goddamn nowhere. Where's your friend? That guy up there in the van gives me the creeps. Are you ready to go?"

"But Mom, I'm supposed to stay for dinner." Her mother pulled out a cigarette and looked back at the house.

"I'm not driving back here in the dark. And you, all by yourself back here. This whole place gives me the creeps." Eleanor had known she would hate Jay's house because the Bruleys were poor in some way that even money couldn't change.

"What's that doing in there?" Her mother was hunched over her match, staring at the hawk.

"Jay's brother caught her."

"It looks like it's bleeding."

"She's okay. Wes—" Eleanor wanted to explain how Wes would tame her. He had the gift. But she remembered the hawk sitting in the bottom of the cage like the sky was crashing down. Her voice choked in her throat. Her mother moved her cigarette to the side of her mouth and looked at Eleanor through the smoke.

"Eleanor, what's going on here?"

"He won't let her go."

"Who won't? Speak up now."

"Wes. The guy in the van."

Her mother looked at her, squinting through the smoke. Eleanor looked back, then away. It was as though her mother was really seeing her and it was scary. She was so used to walking around her edges.

Her mother took a long drag on her cigarette and stamped it out in the grass. Then she reached past Eleanor, pulled the nail out of the hinge and threw the door wide open. The hawk blinked, thrashed her way out of the cage, and flew. Eleanor's mouth went into a big O of protest and awe.

The hawk beat her way across the yard, banked up over the vegetable patch, then over the trees. A few cream-colored feathers blew across the yard and caught on the dandelions. Her mother tossed the nail into the cage.

"Mom. That wasn't your hawk."

"That was nobody's hawk." She sounded like she was ready to cry. "Now get in the car."

Eleanor followed her up to the yard where Wes was rummaging in the back of the van. Her mother swung out of the yard, tires scraping gravel. Eleanor leaned out the window and saw Jay standing on the porch. It was too dark to see her face.

The Heron Path

Eleanor had never been in a pick-up truck before, and it made her nervous that Jay didn't have a driver's license. She had to step up, haul herself in and then lean way out to yank the door shut. The inside of the cab was all metal as though someone had ripped out everything soft and left the rivets behind. The seat had a thin-stretched nylon cover and the springs were just dying to poke up through it. Jay scootched down in the seat and probed around the floor with her feet, then stretched way over to the ignition to start the truck. The engine caught with a ragged series of explosions and a high rubbery whine. The Internal Combustion Engine. The truck was built for people a lot bigger than Jay. She was busy ducking down to grab the stick shift and feeling with her toes for the clutch while trying to keep her chin up over the steering wheel. She drove down the gravel road thrashing like a fish caught in shallow water.

Jay was busy driving and the engine was loud so they rode along without talking. The tires popped gravel into the dusty bushes for a long while until the road softened out with yellowed pine needles and thick brush gave way to open pine woods. Jay was chin up and eyebrows down trying to concentrate on the pine needle track ahead. Then she gave the steering wheel a yank, brought the truck up flush against a tangle of hobble bush and cut the engine.

"We're here. Open up that glove box."

Eleanor pushed the button on the glove compartment a couple of times until it finally gave way and the door popped open. Jay reached across her and took out a flashlight and a pack of Salem cigarettes.

"Here's our treat," she said and stuck her nose in the pack for a good sniff. "Not even stale." Eleanor started to ask where she had gotten them, but decided that if they were stolen, she didn't want to know. Jay put the pack in the pocket of her flannel shirt and flicked the flashlight on and off a few times, aiming it into the dimness under the dashboard.

"Why do we need a flashlight?"

"What if it gets late?" She pulled up on her door handle and jumped down. "You're gonna have to come this way. There's no handle inside on that door." Eleanor slid over the nylon seat, waiting for a spring to pop up and snag her pants. Jay crossed the road and turned to wait by a metal bar that served as a gate across a path.

"Is this someone's private property?"

"Nope. It's nobody's. It's going to be part of a reservoir someday. My house is going to be under that reservoir, too. The state already paid us for the land." Jay was flicking the flashlight on and off, wasting the batteries.

"Your family is going to have to move then."

Jay just shrugged. It was already getting late. Where the sun slanted through the pines, it cast long skinny shadows across the path. Eleanor could hear a steady scrape of grasshoppers up ahead where the woods opened out. The path ended in a place filled with late afternoon light. Two small ponds glowed in the light with an earthen dike running between them. A heron strolled long-legged down the path on the top of the dike, as though sampling the world of humans. Jay stepped forward and the heron glanced back at them. It sulked down the embankment and disappeared into a stand of cattails.

"This is really pretty." The water was smooth pale blues and lavender, skimmed shiny with green lily pads. Mallards dabbled in the open water, green-blue heads catching the light.

"My uncle traps muskrat here."

Eleanor didn't say anything to that. Trapping seemed like a mean thing, but if the uncle was poor, he might need the money.

"He skins them out and sells the pelts. You ever eat a muskrat?"

"No." Eleanor thought of their furless tails.

"They're not as nasty as you'd think. Pa cooked some up one night. I was there when my uncle brought them in, but I'll eat most anything. Pa told me not to tell my brothers. He told them it was pork. So the whole time we're eating supper, Pa's watching Wes and Dale and they're eating just fine. It did taste just like roast pork and I was kinda disappointed. So I says to Pa, not thinking, this tastes just like pork. Well, Dale and Wes stopped eating and looked at Pa. They started yelling, what the heck is this stuff? Pa just looked at me and said, why can't we ever have some peace and quiet here. Then Wes and Dale, even though they were big then, started crying and ran out the door. It sure was funny." Jay smiled for just a second.

They walked along the heron's path. Jay didn't tell any more stories. The mallards made a ripply sound with their bills in the water. A squadron of Canada geese came honking over the pines and dropped into the pond with a lot of splashing and more honking until they settled down. They stopped to watch a white-footed mouse sitting at the end of a log, nibbling a big orange mushroom. It was quiet enough to hear its little teeth clicking. Jay sat at the other end of the log and pulled out the pack of cigarettes. The mouse eyed her and bolted. Jay stuck a cigarette in her mouth and lit it, then leaned her head back to blow out the smoke. From the side, Jay looked almost pretty, with dark eyes and a nice strong chin. She turned and offered the pack to Eleanor.

"Want one?"

"No. My brother gave me one once and it made me sick."

"These are menthol. They taste like peppermint." She handed hers to Eleanor, who took a short puff and coughed. Jay patted her back but handed the cigarette to her again.

"Just take little drags at first. You'll get used to it."

They sat on the log watching the sun turn orange and passing the cigarette back and forth. A few latecomer geese dropped down, braking with their feet on the surface. Eleanor liked the way the cigarette went from Jay's lips to her own.

"Look behind us," Jay said quietly. Eleanor turned. The moon had crept up over the pines while they watched the sun. Now the moon and sun faced each other, east and west. The moon caught the sun's orange light and, for a moment, they were balanced in brilliance. Then the sun slipped behind the pines and the night rightly belonged to the moon.

"The hunter's moon," Jay said. A bat zigzagged over their heads making no sound. A muskrat swam in a purposeful line, neat head breaking the surface and leaving a v-shaped wake that caught moonlight. Jay lit another cigarette but Eleanor waved it away. She felt light-headed and hollow. She watched Jay in the moonlight and breathed in the smoke and the smell of her in the damp air. She noticed how Jay's dark hair curled a little over the worn collar of her shirt.

"Jay, how come you don't let your hair grow out, or just cut it different so the girls don't tease you about it?"

"If they don't make fun of my hair, they'll find something else. I don't care. I turn sixteen in a year and a half and then I'm quitting school, anyway."

Eleanor sat up straight, knowing how Jay's brothers must have felt looking at the meat on their plates.

"You can't quit. You're smart. You're in advanced math. When will I see you?"

"Sixteen, and I'm leaving." She threw the cigarette into the water and it hissed.

"But what about college?"

"What makes you think I want to go to college? Us Bruleys aren't school people."

Eleanor pictured Wes and Dale with their bony legs sticking out from under cars all day. Jay's father whittling a wooden duck in their bare kitchen. What would Jay's place be in that house all day?

"Fine. You hang out with the Bruleys and skin muskrats."

Jay stood up and started walking back to the truck without answering that. The moon was so bright she cast a shadow that lost itself in the water. Eleanor trudged behind her, wanting to pull back her last words.

They climbed into the truck and Jay started the hard-banging engine. She drove, as before, intent on the road and the workings of the truck. But this time it seemed that her concentration was deliberately aimed away from Eleanor. Eleanor took the pack of cigarettes from the seat and lit one. Her stomach felt ready to bolt anyway, and she wanted something to do besides watch Jay's face in the dashboard light. Jay drove with the highbeams on and everything was black outside the sweep of their light. Everything except the moon, which was high now and shining like another headlight.

Snow Geese

Jay sat in the kitchen with her feet up on the bench, trying to keep her eyes on the page. Three chapters, a quiz tomorrow. Out in the parlor, in the slim view she had through the doorway, Pa sat in a rocking chair carving thin shavings from a small block of wood. It would be a green-winged teal when he was finished. Wes and Dale sat watching him at work. Jay could see only their boots, stretched out toward Pa, both pairs shifting one foot over the other.

"You've got to hollow it out good or it's going to ride too low on the water. See?" Pa held the carving out to Wes and Dale and turned it over. Jay watched the two pairs of boots, one foot over the other, then switch again. Wes waggled one foot back and forth.

"The head has to be upright. They look nice and artistic with the neck bent, but no duck swims like that. They keep their heads up straight. Watch one sometime."

Wes's boots hit the floor. "Pa, me and Dale are going out for awhile. Maybe into town, okay?"

Jay went back to her book. Not much in it made sense. Wars in countries that didn't exist. Carthage. Asia Minor. She raised her head again, tried to remember what she had just read. All that came to mind was that the winners of one of those old wars salted the land before they marched home. That seemed more cruel than any war.

Pa came into the kitchen and set the little half-carved teal on the table.

"I'm going to make some tea and then I'm going to bed. Tired." Pa went to bed earlier and earlier. Pretty soon he wouldn't make it through supper. Jay set the book face down and picked up the carving. The bill looked a little heavy. She would have shaved it down, made it more delicate. But Pa was right about the neck. The bird was alert and watchful. A duck in the wild. Pa set two mugs on the table.

"You like him? I'll give him to you when I'm finished. Hunters don't buy wood decoys now anyway. They use the plastic ones. Cheaper. That's why your brothers don't care about learning to carve."

"Teach me. I'll learn."

Pa shook his head. "I'll be glad when we move away from here. The boys don't listen. You run wild in the woods. Sauvage." He growled the word low in his throat, then smiled. "That's your mother's word. Sauvage."

Jay waited for him to say more. It had been a long time since he had talked about her mother. He filled the kettle, set it on the stove and stood staring at it, rubbing at a callous on his thumb.

"What does that mean? So-varge?"

"It's French. It means wild. Like the place your mother grew up, in Quebec. Twenty miles to town. The bridge washed out half the time. She hardly ever went to school. But she didn't want you growing up that way. Woods-wild. Sauvage." The kettle whistled and he poured water into the mugs. "You're named for her, you know. Jeanette. Little Jeanne. Maybe you can go by your real name, now that you're older.

Jay blew across her mug to cool her tea.

"What's the name of the girl who's been coming around here? The red-haired girl."

"Eleanor."

"That's nice. Nice you have a friend, another girl." He picked up his mug of tea and turned to go upstairs. Then he reached down and rubbed his scarred knuckles across the top of Jay's head. "Maybe she can show you how to fix your hair nice. That will be better than carving ducks with an old man."

"You're not old."

"I feel old. Leave a light on for the boys. God only knows when they'll get home."

Jay listened to his footsteps go up the stairs, the clock ticking in the parlor and the wind slapping a loose shingle outside. She stepped out onto the porch, holding the warm mug in her hands. The road was a pale streak in the dark. It was cold now. There was no more cricket noise, or peep toads, or night-calling birds. Just the wind hurrying dry leaves across the yard. The tea steamed in the cold air.

The red-haired girl. Jay thought about Eleanor, thought hard about her walking up the road in the dark. Sometimes when she thought that way about Eleanor, she would look up and Eleanor would be there. Jay closed her eyes, saw Eleanor walking up the road, a soft dark shape sharpening into a long-legged girl with a lop-sided ponytail. But when she opened her eyes, the road was empty. Sheer wanting did not work. Jay knew it never did, it just seemed that way sometimes. Wanting couldn't make anything happen.

Eleanor knew the names of everything. The book names. Common grackle, not just a blackbird. Viburnum. Yellow birch, paper birch, black birch. Once she broke off a twig of black birch and handed it to Jay.

"Taste this. It tastes like mint." It did.

Eleanor knew the names of things that Jay had never wondered at. Bark beetles, twisted stalk. The smooth-barked tree they were sitting in was an American beech. Its branches hung low and wide and were good for sitting on. It was a moonless night, clear with a sky full of stars. The field in front of them glowed in the dark under a thin skim of frost. Jay shoved her hands deep into her jacket pockets and swung her feet to keep them warm. She thought about the warm parlor up the hill, with the wood stove stoked for the night. But she liked it out by Slater's field, sitting in the big beech tree with Eleanor, who was staring out into the field, watchful. Her pale skin was shining in the starlight like she was lit with frost, her head tilted as though she was listening for something far away. She pointed toward the east.

"There's Orion. A winter constellation."

"Wes calls that one the hunter."

Jay didn't much care about the book names for things. She knew the important things. Wes had taught her where to find bird nests, how to touch the edge of a track to feel if it was old or fresh. That white berries were always poisonous. But she liked that Eleanor knew these names, that she carried little guidebooks with her when they walked in the woods.

"Let's watch for shooting stars," Eleanor said.

"If you watch for them, they never happen. You have to be surprised."

"What will happen to all this," Eleanor waved at the field, the woods, "when the reservoir is built?"

"I used to think they would just flood it. That I could come back someday and it all would still be here." Jay closed her eyes in the dark, saw the house, its windows and doors open, deep in green-gold water. "But Wes told me that they'll knock everything down, even the trees."

"And, of course, Wes knows everything." Eleanor slid down off the branch and tugged at the cuff of Jay's pants. "Let's walk, it's cold."

They walked across the field and Jay felt the scrape of old blackberry thorns against her legs. Eleanor walked ahead. Her hair was caught under the collar of her jacket. Jay wanted to reach out and free it, so that it would swing down her back. Eleanor stopped and Jay almost stumbled into her.

"Look."

In the middle of the tangled field was a circle of lacy ferns rimed with frost. It looked like a fairy forest, like magic alive and real in the night. A fox barked across the field, three sharp yips.

"I'm going to miss you when you leave," Eleanor said softly. Then she moved ahead in the dark.

They climbed over a low stone wall into the woods and stepped gently through the crisp leaves, although Jay did not know why they were trying to be quiet. It was darker in the woods. Eleanor tripped and put her hand on Jay's shoulder for a moment to steady herself. Jay put her hands out and felt her way down the path, holding branches back for Eleanor, until they stepped out on the bank of the river. The river was a shining strip of black catching light from the river of stars above it.

"I've never been here at night," Eleanor said.

Jay heard her swallow and could almost feel her stiffen. "It's okay. I know the way."

The path was smooth under her feet and she was moving surely and quickly. The river was a steady rush of sound beside her. She felt that they were going toward something, some place that would disappear if they didn't get there soon. But there was only the path curving along the river to the swimming place.

Jay heard music, a soft wail in the distance that grew loud and insistent. There was a light up ahead, the orange glow of a bonfire. She heard the sound of breaking glass, shouts, a girl's high-pitched laugh. They kept walking toward the noise and light, then Jay stopped and put her hand on Eleanor's arm to keep her from stepping out where they could be seen. They stood on the path under the leafless trees.

It was only a party. Older kids with a loud radio, smashing beer bottles on the rocks. Up ahead, Jay could see the hard little glow of cigarettes and shapes made bigger by shadows lurching around the fire. The bonfire was a high heap of scrap lumber that flared and sparked as it crumpled.

Embers spilled out onto the grass and ignited a little blaze that zipped along the ground like a lit fuse.

Jay and Eleanor stood in the dark and watched hulking shapes stagger in drunken dancing, and bottles catching firelight, raised to faceless mouths. It was only a party, Jay knew. They could even join in, no one would know them in the dark.

It was only the swimming place. Where Jay had first seen Eleanor. A hot summer day. She remembered looking across the river. There she was, wading, bright hair and sunburned shoulders. The swimming place. Where Jay had been heading in the dark, to sit there in the quiet by the water. And maybe tell Eleanor that she would miss her, too.

"They're all really drunk," Eleanor whispered. "Let's get out of here."

But Jay stood there a minute longer, watching someone heave another pile of boards on the fire. The wood caught as though soaked in kerosene and roared up so that the thrower leapt back like a spooked horse. Shadows raced up against the bright trees and flowed back down as the fire died. In the confusion of darkness and music and drunken laughter, two figures stood by the fire holding onto each other. They swayed gently to a slow rhythm in their own circle of music and light.

Jay watched them and something flared inside her, like a warning and a call. She closed her eyes against the light, then opened them and touched Eleanor's hair where it caught the light. When Eleanor turned her head, Jay leaned over and kissed her on the soft smooth place behind her ear.

Eleanor did not move or say anything. When the bonfire flared again, Jay saw her face. She looked startled, like someone awakened by a loud noise. And Jay saw, with sharp regret, fear. The fear in the eyes of an animal just before it bolts. Jay said the only thing she could think of that might take that look away.

"Don't worry. I'll be leaving soon." Jay looked down at the black ground and waited. She still felt a soft warmth on her lips. All the night sounds, the crack of sticks in the bonfire, the wild yells, the river, were far away in the cold night. Inside, she was warm and quiet. She closed her eyes to feel the quiet. A stick cracked under weight, a careless noise. She looked up and saw Eleanor moving ahead of her along the path.

Eleanor stepped into the circle of light around the fire, her back to Jay, her hair still tucked down into her collar. Jay started to follow. Sometimes you have to do one thing to see what happens next. But she had done that one thing and could not stomach risking another. She turned and walked back along the path by the river.

Whatever had guided her feet before was gone. She stumbled over rocks and branches and stubbed a sneakered toe against a rock. She had been in the woods alone at night before and been at ease, at home. Now she slipped and fell twice as she made her way back up the hill. She blundered over the stone wall and a branch slashed her eye. She stumbled across the field, an empty space next to her, and felt the cold damp ferns and grasses soaking her feet.

The next morning, Jay stood on the front porch and watched Wes and Dale trudge over to the van. Her father loaded a table saw into the pickup. It had snowed lightly the night before, the first snow of the season. The sky was carrying more snow. The air was cold and everyone was breathing fog. She watched them drive up the road and stood there while the rest of her breakfast got cold in the kitchen. Any other day, she would turn and go back inside, finish her breakfast, then walk up the road to catch the bus to school. This morning she stood there until she knew the bus had stopped, waited a moment with its doors hanging open, and driven off without her.

She had been alone before, but this morning was different because she should have left. The house and the outbuildings, standing empty and quiet in the day, seemed to have a life of their own. The house was full of clocks ticking and faucets dripping. She prowled the familiar rooms and each chair and lamp and the poker and shovel seemed to have its own separate life.

Out in the barn, old harnesses hung in dusty sunlight. She found a slim pale owl standing in the dimness up in the rafters. Wes had taught her that an owl in daylight was a bad sign. But this one was not flying. That might make a difference.

Outside, the sky was pale and bright like the owl in the barn. The thin snow was crossed by tracks of animals roaming in the night. She remembered Wes teaching her to track animals. Once they had followed deer sign to a thicket where the deer bedded down for the day. They heard soft rustlings as the deer slipped away. Jay had reached down to touch the matted leaves where the deer had been lying and felt the warmth of their bodies.

There were bright orange ribbons tied to a line of trees. The surveyors had come through again, setting the boundary lines for the reservoir. The first time the surveyors had come, she, Wes and Dale had walked from tree to tree, breaking the ribbons and shoving them in their pockets. She had been foolish enough then to think they could stop the reservoir. But the surveyors seemed to have a steady supply of orange plastic ribbon.

The woods were quiet, the ribbons bright against the gray and white tree trunks. She left them alone. A fir had toppled during a storm and torn a big hole in the ground. The exposed roots were shot through with needle frost. Eleanor called it that. Jay had not known that frost had names. Rime frost, hoar frost, needle frost. It wasn't good to think about Eleanor. *I'm going to miss you when you leave.*

Jay would have stayed then and let the water rise up around her. Now one place seemed as good as another.

She turned up the thinly wooded slope that led to Slater's field and the beech grove. It wasn't a good thing to do on this gray quiet day, but Jay kept walking. The field was covered with an even layer of snow, bright under the cloudy sky. It dazzled her eyes and she stood blinking. Geese honked overhead. They were flying in a wedge, one side short and the other trailing out with stragglers. They called to each other, a harsh houck, houck. Jay counted twelve. She could hear their wings whistle.

The wedge dropped and scattered. Jay tilted her head back to watch them come in, shading her eyes with her hand. They landed in the snow, white on white, wings tipped in black. They touched down and rose again, drifting back into a ragged wedge and heading east to the coast. Jay had hoped they would stay.

The Nivean Environment

Snow may be the key to survival or it may be detrimental to the organisms that exist in the snowpack. This snow world is known as the *nivean environment*.

Eleanor walked home in the dark the long way, by the roads. It started snowing, light dry flakes, by the time she reached her house. In the morning, she looked out her bedroom window. The bright snow had drifted over the houses and hedges and made them beautiful. The night at the river seemed far away.

Now that there was snow, she could begin her science project. She had a real experiment for the science fair this year, one where she didn't know the outcome in advance. Last year she had planted coleus plants in different soils: sand, dirt, bits of asphalt. She had known the outcome for those coleus plants, especially the one in the asphalt.

She went out into the new snow to the abandoned orchard in back of the house. She measured and stuck six thermometers into the snow, each at a different depth. She planned to check the temperatures three times a day and note any variations. It made sense to her that they would all be the same temperature. Snow was frozen. Thirty-two degrees. But Miss Duffney said that might not be true.

Miss Duffney, her science teacher, was from Florida. She thought snow was fascinating and talked about winter as though it was some other planet. The kids in the class had shoveled a lot of snow. The next chapter in the textbook was on electricity and most of them wished Miss Duffney would stick with the book.

Eleanor liked the idea that something she had been taking for granted might have surprises. She stuck the last thermometer in the crook of an apple tree to monitor the regular temperature, the ambient air temperature. She noted the location of her thermometers and the air temperature on a clipboard and hoped for unexpected outcomes.

Her mother had supplied the thermometers. She had a new job at Olson's Hardware. It was a temporary job, counting and packing inventory because the store was closing down. Her mother loved the store and the work. She came home late, after Eleanor had eaten dinner by herself, but she was never tired anymore. She liked to sit at the kitchen table at night, while Eleanor washed the dishes, and explain what she had learned about hardware that day. Ballpeen hammers and roofers' hammers, tee joints and elbows. She lined up nails on the table: galvanized, finish, blued drywall, one with tiny rings all along the shank.

"Guess what that one's for. Asbestos shingles!" Next Thursday would be her last day.

She brought Eleanor the thermometers in a waterstained box.

"I asked Alfred Olson straight out if I could have them. I didn't steal them."

The thermometers were attached to strips of tin with decorative flowers and vines painted on them. Eleanor thought the decorative strips might get in the way and they did not look serious enough for science. Her mother took a pair of sharp-beaked pliers—"Tinsnips!"—and trimmed them back.

Eleanor stood at the bus stop that morning and imagined her science project. This one would not be raggedy and last minute. It would be big and clean with neat lettering. She would have charts and graphs. She would display the thermometers with a small sign: Courtesy of Olson's

Hardware. This would give her mother the opportunity to talk with people about hardware. This year, her mother would be at the science fair.

Eleanor felt she could win this year. She wasn't sure what made a winning science project, but she knew it had to be very neat on three white poster boards, not cut from a cardboard box the night before it was due. The bus came and she sat looking out the window at the snow. She pictured herself on stage in the school auditorium, accepting first prize. She knew they usually stuck a blue ribbon on the winning project while the photographer from the town paper took pictures. But maybe this year they would hand out awards at a big ceremony. Her mother would be sitting in front with Miss Duffney, smiling and clapping. She would look up the empty aisle and see her father standing at the back in the big double doors. He would give her a little salute before stepping outside.

Jay would be there in the middle of the cheering crowd. Eleanor would look and look and finally see her. Eleanor accepted the blue ribbon and held it out to Jay across the auditorium. Jay gave her a quick smile. Eleanor rested her head against the bus window, closed her eyes and smiled back. She remembered Jay's kiss by the river. The surprise of it, the warmth, the wondering. What it meant. If it meant. How she had wanted to jump and shout, then fear like a cold hand in the middle of her back marching her away. She had wanted to kiss Jay back, or something like that, something all wrong like that. When she saw Jay at school, she hoped they could make it right again.

Jay was not at school. Eleanor looked for her in the halls all day, then felt strange and shy about taking the bus to her house after school. She rode her own bus home and wished that everything was the way it had been before. When the bus let her out, she ran to the orchard and checked her thermometers. The snow temperatures were all the same. There was nothing to graph yet.

The transmission of heat through a material takes time. This time delay results in a phenomenon in the snowpack called *temperature gradients*.

    The next day it snowed all morning. Jay was not in school again. Eleanor made up her mind to take the bus to Jay's house after school. But when school was dismissed early because of the storm, Eleanor went straight home. She told herself that she needed to check her experiment, that she would ask her mother for a ride to Jay's house later. The snow was drifted to sixteen inches deep in the orchard. The thermometer closest to the ground was two degrees colder than the one at the top of the snow. Three of them were colder than the air temperature.
    Eleanor took off her gloves and noted the temperatures on her chart. The tips of her fingers were white in the cold. She had walked away from Jay and stepped up to the fire, held out her hands as though they needed to be warmed. A boy and a girl, hanging drunkenly onto each other, fell against her. Another boy stood across from her, drunk and unsteady, swaying, and she was afraid he would fall into the fire. She had looked back and Jay was gone.
    She knelt in the snow and re-buried the thermometers, noted their depths on the chart. The snow where she dug was mixed with frozen bits of leaves and the brown scaly covers of apple buds. She remembered something she had not known she remembered. Late fall, not yet winter. The last of the witch hazel blooming, small yellow buds. David sitting in a corner in one of the half-built houses behind the orchard, sobbing. He was not crying the way boys do, the vicious and furtive way they wipe at their eyes. His hands covered his face and he was sobbing loudly. She had heard him and looked for him. Then, finding him there in the corner, she was suddenly embarrassed, ashamed for him.

She hadn't asked him why he was crying. She had walked away. She remembered how she had left him, witch hazel still in bloom along the path. Eleanor brushed snow off her chart, put her gloves on and walked back to the house.

The storm moved off through the afternoon. After dark, the sky cleared and the air was dry. Eleanor walked out to the orchard in the deep powdery snow to check her thermometers again. The ambient air temperature was twelve degrees. She dug down into the snow and checked the temperatures with a flashlight. The ones in the snow were warmer than the air temperature. An unexpected outcome.

She made her notes and re-buried the thermometers. Already, she felt the memory of the night by the river trying to slide away, to become something she might have imagined. She kept pulling it back. She had stood in the dark watching the fire. A foolish and dangerous bonfire in the dry winter woods. Jay had kissed her. But other girls kissed each other, laughed and hugged. But Jay was not other girls.

The house was cold that night. Something was wrong with the furnace. It made a high humming noise while the house got colder. Eleanor made a grilled cheese sandwich and waited for her mother to come home from Olson's.

Her mother was later than usual and came in the door carrying a box of pipe fittings and crying. Olson's had decided to call in something called a liquidator to finish the job. Alfred Olson had given her the pipe fittings and said she was the best little worker he had ever seen. Eleanor decided not to tell her about the furnace or ask for a ride to Jay's house. She wasn't sure what she would say to Jay, anyway. What had really happened?

Eleanor huddled under the covers in bed and tried to read. If something had happened, she should not have walked away. The room was icy. She closed her book and wrapped her hands in the blanket. Maybe Jay was afraid to see her, too.

She shut her eyes and saw snow and ice. She was cold and awake and knew she was not dreaming. It was more like a place she had never seen but knew was there. It was always winter in this place. She and Jay lived in a cave dug into the snow. Jay carved shelves into their snow walls. They skated down the river to buy food and candles and so Eleanor could get books out of the library. The river was always frozen. At night, they lit candles and Eleanor read to Jay until they fell asleep. They slept wrapped in red wool blankets.

Sometimes David came to visit them. He was older now and traveled around the world. He brought them maps and silver jewelry and leather boots. Sometimes Eleanor went with him, and they wore snowshoes and hiked through mountains. When she and David returned, the three of them built a big fire outside and sat up all night telling stories. Jay taught them about the woods. There was always a ring around the moon. Jay said the ring predicted snow.

Eleanor woke up in the night to the sound of hard rain. By Saturday morning, a thin winter fog hung over what was left of the snow. Eleanor pulled on her cold clammy clothes and ran outside. The air was warm and moist, almost tropical. There were big gray puddles in the orchard. The broken old apple trees were black with rain. Her thermometers were scattered in the patchy snow. Two were lying on bare wet ground, stuck with bits of bark and mud. The edges where her mother had cut the metal were already rusting. The experiment was ruined.

```
Organisms are classified according to the
way they experience the nivean environ-
ment. Those that survive, or even thrive
through the winter, are called chionophiles
```

(from the Greek, literally, "snow lovers").

Eleanor stood at the edge of the orchard, holding her ruined thermometers. Everything had failed. Everything was wrong.

She heard an engine and turned to see the van pull up into the driveway. Jay jumped down from the passenger side and trudged towards the side door of the house. The driver's side window rolled down and Dale stuck his head out, said something to Jay, who stopped and stood kicking at the snow. Dale pointed to Eleanor, then stripped the gears as he backed out of the driveway. Jay walked across the yard to Eleanor.

Eleanor waited with her hands full of thermometers. Jay bent down to pick up a handful of sodden snow and squeezed it into an iceball. Her jacket was hanging open and Eleanor noticed that her shirt was buttoned wrong. Jay looked back over her shoulder, as though hoping that the van might still be in the driveway, and Eleanor's own fear seemed small.

"My science project's wrecked."

Jay nodded at the thermometers. "Sorry."

"It's okay. I won't walk away next time?" It come out high and squeaky. A mouse voice.

Jay fired her iceball at an apple snag.

"I won't walk away next time," Eleanor said. Jay looked up and gave her a quick Jay-smile. Eleanor set the thermometers in the crook of a tree and they walked to the river.

The snow was still deep in the woods by the river. Under the trees and willow thickets, there were crazy circles of rabbit tracks and raccoon roamings. Eleanor and Jay stood tossing bits of snow into the swirling water. For the first time, Eleanor noticed that Jay was beautiful. Short and sturdy, her skin the soft color of a sparrow's breast. Her hands looked strong enough to break bones, but the backs of her wrists, sticking squarely out of frayed sleeves, were small, even delicate.

Tiny silver-winged insects hovered in the air. Eleanor wondered where they had come from, in the middle of winter.

"It's the January thaw." Jay said it as though it was something they could count on, year after year. But Eleanor did not believe that anything happened so predictably. Not anymore. There were unexpected outcomes. Charts and graphs were useless.

"Look for a ring around the moon tonight. Then it will snow again," Jay said.

They stood together, listening to the river. Eleanor always wanted to be somewhere else, but at that moment she wanted to be there, at the river with Jay, and nowhere else. It wasn't spring, but it felt like spring. The January thaw. Did it really happen every year? Why had she never noticed?

The river was clear and every stone on the bottom was flecked with light and color. Eleanor saw a blue shell and took Jay's hand, to lean out over the river and reach for it.

Spring Thaw

It is late winter, early spring. The river is free of ice, brimming with snowmelt. It slides along, full-bodied, flowing over its banks. By mid-day, the sun is high over the bare oaks. In the woods, close to the wet dirt and slippery black leaves, the air is still cold. Gray tongues of rain-sodden snow lie in shaded places. Soft-bodied salamanders half wake and grapple their way out of damp leafmold to leave eggs hanging in still pools like a string of blue globes.

Along the river, weary night herons drop down to rest at daybreak and hungry crows pull at a tattered warbler nest. The deep purple hoods of skunk cabbage shelter fragile flowers in half-frozen mud. In backwaters still rimmed with shards of ice, thin-skinned wood frogs hang half-submerged and sing. A great horned owl stands in a wary half-sleep over three owlets who wait hungrily for night. Sap flows from a frost-burst maple. There is nothing tender about spring. The river slides along, rolling heavy stones in the deep current.

Under the Bridge

```
The earth tilts on its axis at an angle of
23 degrees, 27 minutes. This angle re-
sults in a varied amount of insolation
throughout the year which, in turn, de-
termines the seasons. The end of winter
is signaled by the diurnal equalization
of insolation known as the spring equi-
nox. Or by free-flowing rivers and the
return of red-winged blackbirds.
```

    Jay and Eleanor launched the old canoe under the stone bridge on Tunk Hill Road. The river was high, topping its banks. Speckled alder branches trailed in the current.

    They waded out, jeans rolled up to their knees, easing the canoe into the water. The water was cold, full of snowmelt. Eleanor's feet went numb and she watched them move painlessly over the sharp gravel bottom. Her legs were winter pale. Jay's looked dark and strong.

    Jay wedged the lunch bag in the deep V of the bow and motioned for Eleanor to get in. She held the boat steady in the current while Eleanor crept low to the bow seat. The bank dropped off quickly and the canoe rocked over deep water. Jay swung one leg over the gunwale and pushed off with the other, pointing the canoe into the middle of the current.

    Eleanor paddled one side, then the other, but it was the current that carried them out of the cold darkness under the bridge and into the sun. Jay trailed her paddle off the stern, steering past a fallen tree. The brittle canoe soaked up the river. Jay handed Eleanor a bailer cut from a bleach bottle and she scooped water over the side. The river was dark brown with its burden of spring silt.

The paddles were dry and splintery and Eleanor had to keep wetting her hands in the cold water to make a slickness between her skin and the wood. Jay was watching the river run up the sides of her paddle in steep little standing waves. She steered as the river slid them along between clay banks pocked with last year's swallow nests.

The river widened and the current slackened. The sun was high by then. Eleanor turned in her seat to face Jay and leaned back with her elbows against the gunwales. Jay leaned her paddle against the thwart and they drifted. The bow caught on a snag and the current swung the stern downstream. When the snag let loose of the bow, the canoe drifted like that for a while, the stern upstream, Jay and Eleanor facing each other across the thwarts.

Eleanor pulled out the lunch that Jay had packed. Jay took an orange and peeled it. Her thumb burrowed under the peel and lifted it off in big pieces. She split the orange and handed half to Eleanor. The canoe turned like a compass needle in the slow current.

"See that white birch back there?" Jay pointed. "A deer died there. The bones were there all winter, then the river washed them away." Jay looked back at the low gravel bank, studying it. Eleanor wished they hadn't gone by the bone place. It made the river suddenly sad but, of course, it always was.

"Did I ever tell you about what happened to my brother David?" Eleanor leaned over the side and looked down into the dark silty water. The water had been clear then. Winter.

"I know about it." Jay picked up her paddle and made a show of steering them around a snag. "Do you know why he did that?"

"No. But it's okay to ask."

"Do you miss him?"

"Of course. I don't know. For a long time I could hardly remember what he looked like." Only the disturbing surprise of certain things. The way his voice started to seesaw high and low one day. The sudden bony length of his bare feet. The wiry orange sideburns that seemed to appear in one afternoon, when she came home and found him leaning in the kitchen doorway, a stranger using their phone.

"He gave me a pocketknife once for my birthday. I carry it all the time." He brought things home like they were souvenirs. A tin film container, a map of South America. A plastic penny-whistle. Once he had a glassy chunk of rock that he said was coal. She remembered this now. How he showed her her reflection in its shiny surface.

"But he wasn't around much. He was out a lot." First, to get away from Dad. Then to get away from their mother. To get away from the dads playing catch in the street with their boys and the moms sitting on the steps, watching. She had missed him then. It was as though he was out looking for someplace else. Eleanor remembered wishing that he would find that place, and take her there with him.

"Everyone said it was suicide. But I don't know." She had said it. Suicide. The word she was never supposed to think about David. The canoe swirled and she felt her stomach swing.

Jay peeled another orange. "Do you think about your brother a lot?"

"Sometimes. Now." About how it could have been different that day. If she had followed him.

"Sometimes I see myself running down the path to the river that day." The snow was heavy and deep that day. She would have been lifting her knees high to set her feet in his tracks, trying to catch up to him.

"By the time I get to him, he's crouched by the river. His clothes are folded in a pile." He is crying hard like that November day when she found him sobbing and walked quietly away. He's shivering and his skin is blue. It was snowing that day, little needles of ice. There would have been snow caught in his hair and melting on his bare skin.

"I would have taken his jacket and put it over his shoulders."

The canoe caught on a snag in a backwater behind a high bank of tangled willows. It rocked side to side, tethered in the strong current. Jay stepped over the thwart and knelt on the cedar slats on the bottom of the canoe. She reached up and brushed Eleanor's cheeks as though she was crying. Eleanor smelled orange peel on her hands and river water.

Sorting

Eleanor woke up but kept her eyes shut, trying to hold on to the bird dream. She lay still, listening to sleet hitting the window. It was a wonderful dream, real and magical. She was walking by the river. It was warm green spring, not disappointing early spring. Trees had small new leaves and the sun came through their open branches. She was just walking. The river glided along, water running up against the banks with a sound like fingers along a picket fence. The woods were full of bird calls and she was sorting them out. The two-note whistle of the chickadees, the veery's windchime song.

A branch curved over the path ahead and she watched a small bird, some sort of warbler. It hopped along the branch and she could see that it was lime green. It was a bird she had never seen before, a color she had never seen on a bird. The bird stopped, cocked its head toward her. It had a dash of red across its face. It was beautiful, tropical. She wished she had a bird guide. Another bird lit on a branch close to her face. She turned slowly, not wanting to scare it away. This bird was sky blue with pink wing stripes. Another bird she had never seen before. She did not remember these birds from any guide books. Two more flew into a witch hazel bush by the river. One was smooth gray with red streaks and the other was shiny black with gold eyes. She could hear wings fluttering and soft rustlings in the leaves. The woods were full of these beautiful birds without names. She stood still, hardly breathing, only moving her eyes. More birds. One cherry red with an emerald tail, one pale yellow with blue wings. What were they? Why had she never seen them before?

"I must bring Jay here to see them." The sound of her own voice had woken her up.

She opened her eyes and the squat dresser and her scattered clothes took their shapes. Sleet hissed and melted on the window. The room was too hot and her throat was dry. She listened for her mother. Dishes clinked at the end of the house. She was up already then, in the kitchen. Eleanor got up, pulled on jeans and a jersey, and splashed water on her face at the bathroom sink. She walked barefoot to the kitchen.

Her mother was sitting at the kitchen window, her back to Eleanor. She was smoking a cigarette and feeding peanuts to the squirrels. Cold air blew across the kitchen from the open window and Eleanor breathed it in. The squirrels jumped and clung to the window sill one after another. Eleanor watched one scrabble at the sill, riffling her tail. Beads of sleet glittered on her gray face. Her mother held out a peanut between her thumb and index finger. The squirrel reached out slowly, shyly, her small paws like hands. She grabbed the peanut, whirled and leapt. Her mother turned.

"You shouldn't be walking around in bare feet. You'll catch cold."

"It's too hot in here."

"There might be broken glass."

"I'll get my sneakers."

"You're going to miss the bus."

"It's Saturday."

Her mother turned back to the window.

"Look at them. See the new one? With the big white tufts on his ears? I call him Jasper. Doesn't he look like a Jasper? I haven't seen Brassy around today. Hope nothing's happened to him."

"Probably sleeping in. Did you leave me any coffee?"

"You're too young to be drinking coffee."

Eleanor rinsed the pot and spooned coffee into the basket.

"I'm going to Jay's house."

Her mother shut the window.

"You're over there more than you're here lately. I found a speck of cereal in that box this morning. I don't know why you kids—why you—keep putting empty boxes back on the shelves."

"Can you give me a ride?"

"You know, when I find a job, I'm not going to be at your beck and call every time you need a ride." The coffeepot started to wheeze.

"I'll be driving myself by then."

"You better watch it, girl, if you want any more rides from me." Her mother got up and started rinsing dishes in the sink. She was wearing faded blue pajama bottoms, a wrinkled blouse and summer sandals. The thick yellow skin on her heels was dry and cracked. Eleanor wished she would just get dressed in the morning.

"I'm thinking about going through David's room. Give some of his clothes to that children's home over in West Bay. Shame to let things go to waste."

"Today?"

"Might as well. Should have done it two years ago."

"I'll help."

"You don't have to. I can get the bags out to the car myself."

"I said I'll help."

Her mother opened David's bedroom door. Eleanor stood behind her with a mug of coffee. She wondered if her mother had been in David's room since the day they took his suit out of the closet. It looked like she had been in at least once—the bed was stripped. The bare mattress had a soft low swing in the middle as though someone had risen from it earlier in the morning.

Eleanor had been in David's room once, the day after the funeral. There had been a glass on his dresser, half full of water, and a folded dollar bill. As though he would step into the room any minute to drink his water and shove his money into his pocket. The room still smelled like him then. Sweat, shampoo, damp wool. She had come in to see what the room would look like without David.

Her mother flipped on the light.

"Well, let's get busy." Her mother snapped a bag open and walked to the closet.

He had taken down his airplanes one day. Little yellow flecks of scotch tape on the ceiling marked where they had hung for years. The closet door was open, his shirts hanging on the knob. His dresser drawers were askew. The dresser was still cluttered with little cellophane stars and flags, insignia for model airplanes. A hardened drop of clear glue held tiny air bubbles. There were fake coins from the summer carnival, twisted paper clips and a red horseshoe magnet. A transistor radio without its plastic back. Eleanor wondered what they would do with it all. The water glass and dollar bill were gone.

"We'll make two piles of clothes," her mother said. "The nice things I'll take to West Bay. The raggedy things. Well."

Her mother didn't know what to do with it all either. How could they throw David's things away? What things in this room had he loved?

"I came in here right afterwards. Looking for drugs. There had to be some kind of a reason." Her mother fingered the collar of a shirt. "This is almost brand new."

Eleanor opened the top drawer. Boys' underpants, the thick waistbands gone soft and loose. Gym socks with bits of gray elastic sticking out of the ribbed cuffs. Holey undershirts. She felt embarrassed. He would not want anyone to see these things. She pulled them out in fistfuls, not looking, and threw them into a bag.

The next drawer was full of jerseys that she put on the bed for West Bay. The third drawer had a tangle of sweaters, a navy blue knit cap, a pair of plaid swim trunks. She remembered them. David jumping off the dock in them. Skinny. There should be more. Something she had never seen. Something that would explain him.

The bottom drawer had gloves with the fingers unraveling. A pair of cutoffs with the back pocket ripped off, leaving a bright new patch of blue denim. In the back of that drawer she found a small velvet jewelry case. David's cufflinks. Gold-colored with small blue stones. A Christmas present one year. She remembered her mother saying to her father, "Now what's a kid need with those?"

Her mother was folding shirts and stacking them on the bed. Eleanor looked at the cufflinks. Jay would like them. She slipped the box into the pocket of her jeans. Her mother continued folding shirts. Her face had a distant determined look. Eleanor remembered that look. Her mother's face bent over David's scraped knee one day, scrubbing out bits of sand and asphalt while he cried.

"He's got a big box of toy planes under his bed," her mother said, without looking up. "I might as well take them to West Bay, I guess. Kids will play with those, won't they?"

"Sure, Mom."

Her mother sat on the bed and wove a tie in and out of her fingers.

"I loved David very much. You know that."

"I know, Mom."

"They always blame the mother." She looked up. Pale blue eyes, pale lips. Eleanor looked back at her. A tired woman wearing pajama bottoms and jaunty sandals. She had not looked at her mother for a long time. Maybe never. Not like this. The faint lines across her forehead, the big smooth curves of her ears. She had not combed her hair. It was pulled back into a loose knot and stray wiry hairs stuck out from her temples and at the back of her neck. Dry knobby hands. No wedding ring. When had she stopped wearing it?

"I don't blame you, Mom."

"I'm almost through with his closet." She slipped David's jacket off a hanger and took the sleeve between her thumb and fingers. "Feel how thin this is, Eleanor. His winter jacket. He never said he was cold. But he must have been, wearing this."

Eleanor took the velvet case out of her pocket, lifted the lid and held it out to her mother.

"Can I take these?"

"Of course. Take something for a remembrance. There'll be other things someday. Things I'm saving. Pictures. For when you grow up." Her mother stood stroking the jacket and gave Eleanor a level look. "When you grow up. I don't want you to dwell on these things now. You're young. You should be happy."

Eleanor held the cufflinks up to the light.

"I want to give these to Jay."

"What will she want with boys' cufflinks?"

"She'll just like them."

Her mother opened her mouth as if to say something. Eleanor snapped the case shut and held her breath. Her mother folded David's jacket and patted it down into a bag.

"Is your coat warm enough? You tell me if it isn't. I'll find the money." She rolled down the top of the bag and handed it to Eleanor. "Help me bring this stuff over to West Bay and I'll drive you to your Jay's house."

Leaving

It had been happening for so long, in small and large ways, that when the day finally came, Jay did not feel it was real. Surely the next morning she would wake up in the familiar shape of her room, the pine grove framed in the window, crows cawing from the roof of the barn.

Leaving was too simple. Carry the last bag of clothes down stairs and out to the van. Climb up into the seat and pull the door shut. Dale turned the key in the ignition, backed out of the yard and drove up the road. Brittle milkweeds and asters scratched at the sides of the van like kitten claws until they pulled out onto Route 44. Past the mailbox that still had their name on it.

Pa had stayed behind to lock up before following in the pickup truck. Jay had asked him why he would bother to lock the empty house and barn and did not see Dale's sad shake of the head until it was too late.

"Dale?"

He was driving with one hand on the steering wheel, leaning against the door, resting his chin in his other hand.

"Do you think Pa will be okay riding by himself?"

"Sure. He has lots of goodbyes to think about."

Eleanor had walked up the road that morning, looking back once to wave. Then she had tucked her hands deep into her pockets and hunched up her shoulders like someone walking against a cold steady wind. Up in Slater's field, she had given Jay her jackknife. *I can't take this. Then what will you have?*

"You crying, Jay?"

"Nope."

"Go right ahead. There's a whole box of kleenex behind that seat."

Leafless trees went by in a gray watery blur. There were fewer houses as they drove north. Low hills covered in bare woods looked like porcupines.

Eleanor had unfolded a map. *Show me where you'll be.*

Way up here.

That's not so far.

Yes it is.

Hawks come down through there in fall. From Canada. The Atlantic Flyway. And snow geese and herons. They'll fly right over you. Then over me. And the stars will be the same. In spring all the snow up in the mountains will melt down into these rivers. See how they flow, north to south? Some of it must come down here.

But I won't be here.

I know.

"I did all my crying last night," Dale said. "Out in the barn. I figured I'd need to be able to see the road this morning. I'm going to miss the barn."

"I'm going to miss the river."

"How about Eleanor?"

Jay nodded but wasn't sure Dale saw. He was passing a truck hauling a load of pine logs.

"Hurts a lot," he said after he got around the truck. "It'll hurt later on, too. Just not as often."

"How do you know?"

"You and her were good friends, huh?"

"The first time I saw her, she had a big magnifying glass and was looking at bugs and things in the river."

"She going to be some kind of a scientist?"

"I guess."

"What are you going to be?"

"Lonesome."

"Talk to me about her anytime you want. Tell me what she was reading in those books she was always lugging around."

"I don't want to talk about Eleanor. It makes me start crying again."

"Well, don't just forget her. Okay?"

"Okay."

Jay cried again for awhile, wiping her eyes on her sleeve. Dale finally reached behind her and put the box of kleenex up near the stickshift. The highway was getting steeper now and they could look down at church steeples and smokestacks in the towns below.

"We'll go fishing up there, Jay."

"Is there a river?"

"Of course. There's rivers everywhere. All one river, you look at a map."

"That's what Eleanor says."

"What else does she say?"

"She knows the names of everything. Water striders, rime frost, cedar waxwings..." Jay leaned her head against the window of the van and closed her eyes. She was tired and her eyes burned with salt. They were climbing now, up into the mountains. *Hemlock, balsam fir. Ravens. The red November berries of mountain ash.*

Wilderness

If you stay I will teach you how to live. I will show you what is real, take you to the wilderness places so you will know what to do with fire and ice. Have you ever held a wild bird in your hand? They are warm and lighter than you would think possible. Under the smooth feathers their bones are hollow and fragile, but the wings are strong enough to break your hold. Have you tried to hold a wet frog? Hand to hand and back again, trying to keep but not to crush? Or made a lantern with your hands full of fireflies, light breaking out between your fingers, fireflies tapping on your palms?

What I am trying to tell you is that everything is constantly changing. You will always be holding and letting go. Pay attention. Be reckless and careful.

Go to the river in winter. Take large stones and throw them onto the ice. They should hit and skitter along leaving a sharp white line. Topple an old snag onto the ice and it should make only one noise when it falls. Only then, go out onto the ice with your hot bare feet and dance.

EPILOGUE ~ 1988

Outliers

"So if the material tells you, 'It may be this,' allow that. Don't turn it aside and call it an exception, an aberration, a contaminant... That's what's happened all the way along the line with so many good clues."
  -Geneticist Barbara McClintock
  A Feeling for the Organism

"It's dark out, Professor Brownell. Why don't we just take some measurements tomorrow at the pond near South Campus?"

"I know it's gotten late. But because the Still River Reservoir is not a naturally formed body of water, it has a unique sub-surface topography. That makes the temperature stratification more pronounced, and there are a few places that generally yield some unexpected data."

"But it's so cold outside."

I am always surprised at my students' lack of enthusiasm for field work. They like it in theory, but the reality of cold feet and wind chill makes them long for the comforts of the lab. Over the years, I have noticed that each class is more awkward in the woods than the last. I've watched my students get progressively clumsier at climbing fences and crossing streams. It's as though they have spent their outdoor time in well-groomed parks, not real woods. They are leery of the woods at night and freely admit to their fears, even the boys. I suppose that is a good thing. But it saddens me that most of their experiences in the woods have been bracketed points in time—summer camp or an Outward Bound session. Each year, fewer of them have spent time in the woods on their own.

Now they tumble out of the van and fumble in the cold with flashlights and notebooks. I suggest that they switch off the flashlights and let their eyes become accustomed to the dark. It's a clear night, but they want their lights. I unlock the gate in the chain link fence that guards the reservoir and lead them down a stony path to the water. The ice is thick this year. They will be able to collect data at several points well off shore.

My students know the routine after this full day of field work. They fan out across the ice in teams of two and begin drilling holes in the ice. When they drill through, water gushes up over the ice as though released under pressure. Later, I will ask them why this happens. Not because it has any bearing on our subject, but because I am always amazed at the range of answers I receive, the fabulous ways that these scientists-to-be construct their world in the absence of hard data.

I walk from one team to the next, helping them to recalibrate the dissolved oxygen meters and encouraging them to be precise in their measurements. I also encourage them to look up from their work to admire the stars. They cast their eyes up obediently, then lean their heads back in open-mouthed awe.

The stars are thick and bright in the winter sky. Here below, there is only the pale ice and the bare black trees. The students flick off their flashlights, one by one, to stand in the dark and watch the stars. Then the flashlights go on again, one by one, and my students bend their heads to their work. They record their measurements on clipboards, then we all troop back to the van.

Tomorrow, in the warmth and light of the lab, we will graph the data, this night's haul of information. In any statistical sampling, there are data points—measurements, events, dates—that lie outside the thickly occurring average. These points are the dots on the edges of the graph, like horizon stars strayed far from the clustered Milky Way.

My students will be dismayed at those data points that do not conform to the statistical trend. They will disregard them as aberrations, deviations from the cool clear path to the answer. But they exist, those outliers, stubborn sparks living on the margins.

My students will ask if they should leave these stray data points out of their calculations. But it is to these outliers that I will send them again, to find out what marvelous events are happening there. It is in these outliers, I will tell them, as I tell them every year, that we find the fullest expression of nature, her wildest strivings and most daring artistry.

Baptism

Mornings in the mountains were sudden. The sun came up over the rounded peaks called The Twins and light fell down into the valley. It was day.

Jay opened her eyes in the brightness. She reached to click off the alarm clock before it rang. She preferred waking to the light but had not wanted to take the chance of over-sleeping this morning.

It was good to wake up in the cabin with the ravens yelling and joyful far off in the woods. She liked the way the sunlight came through the big front window of her cabin, cut for a tourist's view of the Franconia Range. Now the old valley cabins were cheap rentals for the locals, and the tourists stayed up at the ski area. The early sun lit up the pale wood shavings on the floor and the half-carved block of wood in its vise, waiting for her.

Most mornings, she started working right away, standing barefoot on the cold plank floor, working herself from dreaming to wakefulness. It was in this half-sleep that she could best follow the grain in the wood, feel how it needed to be carved, find the balance of pressure and restraint in her hands.

She pulled on a flannel shirt and sweatpants and stood running her hand over the still-rough scales of a trout in yellow birch. Her pencil sketch for this carving had looked good, the trout strong and leaping. She had imagined the forceful feel of its muscles in the wood. Now she wasn't sure. The trout she knew were quiet down in deep pools, breathing cold water through delicate pink gills. Was this leaping trout just a city man's version? One that would sell? She would finish it, nonetheless. Once she had a roughed-out carving of the face on any of her animals, she could never bring herself to toss them on the kindling pile. When she finished this one, she decided, she would carve another trout in poplar or ash, weightless and waiting and still.

But even the leaping tourist-trout would have to wait this morning. She walked away from her work and headed for the shower. Family obligations. Not always convenient, but it was an odd comfort to know that her presence at certain events was precious and necessary. Wes and Sharon's wedding. Dale's graduation. In return, they—Sharon, Wes, Dale, her father—showed up dutifully at her first opening, frowning at people who fingered her work. They themselves had stood with their hands in their pockets, sometimes reaching out to turn over a price tag and raise their eyebrows at what people would pay for Jay's wooden animals.

And pay they did, to her own surprise. She had done well at this year's Labor Day craft show. She took off the flannel shirt and stepped into the shower. She lifted her face to the spray, shut her eyes and calculated how much she had sold over the summer. She would still have to work timber this winter with her father. He needed her help anyway.

She soaped her hands and ran them over her arms and chest. She would have to call the woman who painted flowers in watercolors. The woman who had given her a business card at the Labor Day weekend show and mentioned a joint show for the holidays. Jay stood so that the shower spray hit the back of her neck and watched the water run down her body. She looked good, strong. Woodcarving had given her arms heft and tightness. She hadn't liked the woman's paintings at first. They were like illustrations in a botany book. But by the end of the weekend, Jay had liked them for that very reason. For their delicacy, precision and accuracy. The woman had been like that, too. Slim, direct. Long, wind-chapped hands. Jay stepped out of the shower into the cool air. She rubbed a rough towel across her shoulders. Yes. She would talk with the woman with the watercolor flowers.

Wes's wife Sharon was Catholic and the baby, Matthew, was going to be baptized today in her family's church. They had chosen Jay, to her surprise, to be the godmother. A role, she thought, that required a wand and gauzy gold skirts or, at least, a husband.

Jay drove up through The Notch. Above treeline, ice gleamed in the deep-cut ravines. Already, in mid-September. She hoped she was dressed right for the occasion. Her father and brothers had it easy. They could put on a tie for instant respectability. She had tried to do the same with a skirt but ended up looking like the rugged women selling potatoes by the roadside over the Maine border. She finally had settled for black slacks and a white shirt.

She arrived at the church early and paced the parking lot and sidewalk. Sharon and Wes arrived next with Matthew, who was crying mightily and was wrapped in a long lacy cloth like an old wedding veil. Wes saw the puzzled look on Jay's face and explained that the cloth had been Sharon's christening gown.

"It's a family heirloom. I hope Matt doesn't spit up on it. He's been kind of fussy this morning."

Wes held Matthew to his shoulder and slow-danced him in a little circle until he stopped crying. Sharon went in to talk with the priest. Jay was relieved to see that Sharon was wearing slacks. But hers were pale blue and matched a little jacket trimmed with white piping. She was wearing pale blue high heels.

"Sharon looks nice," Jay said.

"She likes to dress up when she can." Sharon was the county game warden, a job that came with a uniform.

"So what does a godmother do at the christening?" Jay asked. "Grant wishes or something?"

"Beats me. The priest will tell you. I think you just have to repeat what he says."

"But the serious part—that I'm responsible for Matt if something happens to you and Sharon. Sharon has a married sister. Are you sure about me?"

"We're sure." Wes smiled and slipped Matthew into her awkward arms. "Here. Just in case, you better get some practice."

Later, Jay remembered the christening like a relief carving, a tableau in dark oak. The high-ceiling church, the young priest in his stiff collar. Her father, solemn and—she saw for the first time—old. With one heavy veined hand clasping a thick wrist. Dale standing beside him, his old suitcoat tight across his shoulders, his hair tamed with water. At the center, Wes and Sharon holding Matthew over the round baptismal font, a corner of the old christening dress hanging in the shallow water. Then Sharon's family, comfortable in their familiar church, Sharon's mother reaching out to touch Matthew's small bare foot.

Jay expected that the priest would lower Matthew into the water but he did not. He said a few soft words, scooped the blessed water in his hand and poured it, almost playfully, over Matthew's fragile forehead. Matthew blinked and opened his mouth as if to cry. Then he pushed at the air with his lace-edged hands and looked out at them all, eyes alert and wondering.

Reservoir

If you look at a map of southern New England, you will see a small blue body of water with the designation Still River Reservoir finely printed in the unadorned typeface of modern cartography. This body of water is new to the landscape, geologically speaking. Although many of the current inhabitants of the area around the reservoir cannot remember when it was not there. It is the old Still River, restrained by a dam, drawn up through intake works, and carried to a filtration plant that strains the last bits of life out of it before it is piped away.

The dam was completed on April 8, 1972, and the diverter that had turned the river from its course during construction was closed. The Still River filled its old course again. Not as dramatic a moment as you might think. A day of slow water motion viewed by surveyors and engineers, all more intent on the intake works and the dam than the river. A day of slow water motion that had begun much earlier in the season.

That spring, as they did every year, the river waters began in the melting of the snowfields in the mountains north. The water flowed south, gathering its spring burden of snowmelt and silt. Runoff poured into streams that became rivers, rivers that became the Still River. At the new dam, currents swirled back into deepening eddies. The river rose up out of its banks past the spring high water mark of tangled black grasses caught half-way up alders and willows. It slid outward through the woods, creeping across stubble fields and filling first seeps and swales, then cellar holes and the empty foundations of barns and sheds. The river flowed around fence posts and washed over stone walls, dissolving boundaries. And finally up high granite ledges with tough bits of juniper growing in dry cracks. The river, drawn up like a blanket over the quiet landscape. The reservoir.

A crow flying over and looking down into the reservoir would see the neat right angles of human design shimmering in the green-gold shafts of light, waiting under the water like some New England Atlantis. The people who could tell that crow how they lived within those carefully crafted squares are gone. But the river is still there, in name and memory.

It's winter again, a cold clear night. Come out on to the ice. Look. The stars are separated by such black emptiness that the laws of astronomy and physics make perfect sense: light years, black holes, infinity. The snow is deep and crusted over, crystals sintered into a glossy shell. The polished surface of the snow reflects starlight through thin cold air into the black sky. What warmth there is on this night is buried in snow. Deep in the snow is where heat is remembered.

Snow remembers. In spring, meltwater cuts through the heavy old banks of snow. The snow is dark with pollen and bits of leaves and dirt. It no longer reflects the light. It absorbs the light, heats and melts. It runs from thin seepages into icy rivulets, brooks, streams and to the river. The river becomes a reservoir of meltwater and snow memories. Winter seals them under the ice.

Under the ice, a pale thin boy swims, gliding by the empty foundations. Copper hair flows around his head, weightless. He swims with smooth powerful motions. A flick of shoulders and he is moving over the gravel road that is still faintly incised on the bottom of the reservoir. He follows it to the old tarmac highway which is crumbling under the pressure of deep water. He swims past an open place where the white bones of a deer are sunk into sand.

Fish breathe softly in the protection of the deer's curved ribcage, gills flashing rainbow light.

Ice is thick over the reservoir. The sky is black and weighted with stars. The ice glows in starlight with the silvery live glow of a pearl. Two young women step out onto the ice carrying sticks and branches. They arrange the wood on the ice in a neat pile. The smaller one strikes a match off her boot buckle and lights the wood. The two girls have been working hard—gathering branches, breaking them, carrying them. Their bodies are hot in the cold air and send out streamers of vapor like seasmoke. They take off their heavy boots and thick socks and begin to slide on the ice leaving long slick trails of meltwater. They hook arms and swing each other around and around. They jump and holler. Others join them, stepping out of the snow-filled woods, spinning, sliding and holding onto each other.

Under the water, the boy rolls onto his back and glides along looking up at the ice. He can see the orange glow of the fire and the red soles of bare feet streaking across the ice. He kicks his own white feet, one strong thrust, and rises slowly. Another frog-like kick and he's moving to the surface, drawn to the colors. He touches the smooth underside of the ice and bends his head back to look. The stars through the ice have pale haloes around them. The sky is full of light. His pale face is turned up and slightly to the side. His mouth is open in amazement. That is how the first sliding dancer sees him, a living eye glowing beneath the ice.

You take what you have, what you always carry, maybe it's just a pocketknife. You chip through the ice, slivers flying like cold sparks. The others kneel beside you and work. You break through to the black water and plunge your hand down, reaching, groping, hoping he is still there.

There are other hands, reaching down with you to pull the boy up out of the water. He is shivering, lying naked and blue-veined on the ice, water running from his mouth. He looks in amazement at the stars. Hands reach out to gently chafe his arms and legs to warm him. Then, finally, you wrap him in your jacket and take him home.

Corvid Press is a small independent literary press.

Corvids are a family of birds — the crows, ravens, magpies and jays — known for their boldness, beauty and intelligence. We publish work that has those same qualities.

CORVID PRESS

Beverly, Massachusetts

www.corvidpress.com